From the day in sixth grade when I discovered *Oliver Twist*, to the December evening I saw Alistair Sim in *A Christmas Carol*, to the weekend I devoted to the Royal Shakespeare Company's eight-hour production of *Nicholas Nickleby*, I've loved Dickens in any shape or form: musicals, TV, movies, books. When I heard about the **TREASURED TALES** month for **LOVESWEPT**, I instantly asked if I could revive one of Dickens's most romantic heros, Sydney Carton in *A Tale of Two Cities*.

I've been in love with this wastrel-hero forever. This hard-drinking, cynical attorney is redeemed by his love for a woman he adores but feels he cannot have. He even goes to the guillotine so she and her family can escape revolutionary France. Bravely mounting the scaffold, he speaks the immortal words, "It is a far, far better thing that I do, than I have ever done. . . ."

"But wait!" I hear you cry, "you can't have the hero die at the end of the book!" Of course not. That was half the fun of writing *Renegade Ways*. But don't flip to the end of the book to find out how I resolved this dilemma. Instead, start where *A Tale of Two Cities* has always begun: "It was the best of times, it was the worst of times. . . ."

Terry Lawrence

WHAT ARE *LOVESWEPT* ROMANCES?

They are stories of true romance and touching emotion. We believe those two very important ingredients are constants in our highly sensual and very believable stories in the *LOVESWEPT* line. Our goal is to give you, the reader, stories of consistently high quality that may sometimes make you laugh, sometimes make you cry, but are always fresh and creative and contain many delightful surprises within their pages.

Most romance fans read an enormous number of books. Those they truly love, they keep. Others may be traded with friends and soon forgotten. We hope that each *LOVESWEPT* romance will be a treasure—a "keeper." We will always try to publish

LOVE STORIES YOU'LL NEVER FORGET
BY AUTHORS YOU'LL ALWAYS REMEMBER

The Editors

Terry Lawrence

Renegade Ways

BANTAM BOOKS

NEW YORK · TORONTO · LONDON · SYDNEY · AUCKLAND

RENEGADE WAYS

A Bantam Book / January 1993

If you would be interested in receiving protective vinyl
covers for your Loveswept books, please write to this address
for information:

Loveswept
Bantam Books
P.O. Box 985
Hicksville, NY 11802

ISBN 0-553-44304-6

Published simultaneously in the United States and Canada

PRINTED IN THE UNITED STATES OF AMERICA

OPM   0 9 8 7 6 5 4 3 2 1

One

It was the best of times, it was the worst of times.

Nick grinned. "Really, Harry, everyone knows this bit," he muttered to himself. Ciphering wasn't much of a challenge when Harry sent Dickens in code.

Nicholas Atwell, third secretary to the British ambassador in Lampura, a tiny island nation south of Ceylon, sighed as an assistant secretary dared slip a paper onto his hideously messy desk. It was a sub-executive order. He signed it and continued decoding the cable from Harry in Patagonia.

It was the age of wisdom, it was the age of foolishness.

Nick wondered if this was Harry's way of saying 'straighten up and fly right, old chap.' In code, of course. Well-meaning people often tried to reform Nick. Thanks to his easy charm and nimble manners, they seldom succeeded.

We had everything before us, we had nothing before us.

"A bit on the grim side, eh, Harry?" he murmured.

It wasn't Harry's fault. Equally bored on the opposite side of the globe, he couldn't very well take the blame for Nick's malaise.

"Malaise," Nick exclaimed, instantly setting to

work on rhyming it with "bordelaise," when a knock on his door ruined his concentration. He set aside the cryptographic, slightly pornographic limerick he'd decided to grace Harry with by return diplomatic pouch, and looked up.

George Cunningham, Foreign Office liaison and front office spy, stood in the doorway rocking on his heels and smiling faintly. "Think you could spare a moment, Nick?"

"I was born to spare moments, George. What is it?"

"Pop in and see the old man, will you? He's got a visitor with a rather tricky problem."

Anything more complicated than opening mail was tricky for Ambassador Whitcraft, a ruddy-faced career foreign service officer who, despite his name, lacked both wit *and* craft.

Nick rose, running a hand through his hair. In pursuit of a neat, sleek look, he managed to dislodge one heavy black lock across his forehead and thoroughly muss the thicket the rest of it had become.

"Getting a bit long for the diplomatic scene," George suggested tactfully.

"It gets wavy in this heat," Nick retorted, haphazardly knotting his tie as he passed the bronzed mirror beside the door. "Too lazy to get it cut, actually." But George was long gone and duty called; Nick had an ambassador to rescue.

And, as Harry had so helpfully pointed out, at this precise moment, posted to this particular dot on the Indian Ocean for three long years with no promotion in sight, Nick had nothing else before him, absolutely nothing at all.

Nevertheless, it wouldn't do to appear overly eager.

He sauntered down the long hall toward the ambassador's office, pausing just once to pick up a flat silvery thumbtack and stick it in the world map on the embassy wall—obliterating the tiny island nation of Lampura completely.

• • •

If not his entire foot, the ambassador had most of his toes in his mouth when Nick entered. Whitcraft's face turned ruddier by the moment as he struggled manfully to extricate himself from a diplomatic quagmire of euphemisms and pseudo-sincerity.

"Miss Hennessy, we appreciate the difficulty this incident must have presented for you and your family all these years, however—"

"Difficulty? Incident? My father's been held hostage for ten years in this country. First by the government, then by the rebels—"

American, Nick immediately noted as he slipped through the teak door. He'd resettled his wrinkled suit on his broad shoulders and used a bright red silk handkerchief to dust off his shoes before entering, stuffing the dirty end back in his breast pocket. He left a jaunty petal or two peeking out.

He might as well not have bothered. The American woman barely noticed him, intent as she was on regaining her composure. She picked up a handbag and searched through it for a tissue, dabbing at the perspiration on her forehead.

She cooled her temper more rapidly than her cheeks. They were flushed and pink. Her eyes, when she turned them Nick's way, were shimmery and green.

His heart hopped like a cricket ball but his smile remained as blandly helpful as he could make it. She had auburn hair the color of cinnamon bark. Damp tendrils clung to her neck. One wispy strand stirred slightly on her cheek as the overhead fan stirred the humid air.

Responding to the ambassador's meek, mute appeal for help, Nick placed one hand lightly on the back of the lady's chair and leaned over, graciously preventing her from rising. He extended his hand.

"You must be Constance Hennessy. Nicholas Atwell, third secretary. I am so very sorry about your father."

"Thank you."

Her hand rested in his. For a moment he wished he could lift it to his lips, but this was the British Embassy, not the French. He held her fingers instead, his thumb lightly grazing the backs of her knuckles. He left it to her to remove it.

"You've heard of my father," she said, her voice warm but strained.

"Who hasn't?" He shrugged, careful not to be flippant or offensive, mindful that she might mistake it as a sign to remove her hand.

She didn't. In fact, her thumb curled around the underside of his fingers and pressed slightly, a silent thanks for his concern.

She wore a floral scent, so much lighter than the heavy tropical flowers growing outside the ambassador's open window. Standing over her, Nick suddenly, passionately wished to bow more deeply, to press his nose into the richness of her hair, to kiss an earlobe in which a tiny diamond stud was embedded, to find traces of more perfume, and kiss them away.

Good heavens. He was either more bored, more desperate, and more rocky than he'd feared, or she was simply the most beautiful, self-possessed, vulnerable, *desirable* woman he'd ever met.

Finally letting go of her hand, he smoothed his tie down his shirtfront to reassure himself his heart wasn't about to jump out of his chest.

He discreetly cleared his throat. "Your father, I'm sorry to say, has been an international *cause célèbre* for more years than I, or the ambassador, have been stationed here in Lampura."

The removal of responsibility from the British Embassy was so neatly done, the ambassador sighed.

Nick felt uneasy that Constance Hennessy had

heard that sigh. She leaned back in her chair, loosely laced her fingers in her lap, and studied him. Nick glanced at the ambassador for permission.

"Of course, of course, do sit down," Ambassador Whitcraft almost pleaded.

Nick slid into the seat opposite the woman and plucked at the woefully wilted crease in his slacks, then crossed his legs. "You were saying, Miss Hennessy?"

"Connie, please."

He smiled.

She nodded civilly, then turned back to the ambassador, determined, dignified, letting her soft green eyes do all the imploring.

Nick's heart squeezed like a fist. He made a mental note to mix more quinine with his gin and tonics from now on. He must have malaria. Since his posting he'd half expected to catch a tropical disease—which was a damn sight more likely than falling in love.

Yet he found himself leaning forward to be closer to her. "Do forgive me for interrupting, I realize this can't be easy."

"It's all right," she replied somewhat hastily. He wouldn't distract her with charm, Connie thought firmly. Although the charm was considerable.

She bit her tongue and reminded herself she couldn't afford to alienate anyone in this country. Years of civil war had caused the major powers to close their embassies. Only the British remained on the island. She needed these Brits as allies. After all, she was on shaky ground as an American. They owed her nothing. Now if she and her father were British subjects . . .

"I'm sorry," she said. "It's been such a long, hard time for my family. My father was imprisoned by the government ten years ago then held hostage by rebels when they took over."

"Three revolutions ago," Nick murmured.

"Yes. Since the British Embassy is the only major Western diplomatic power still here, I can only turn to you. You must have some influence, if not with the rebels, then with the government."

"The governing *du jour*." Nick pursed his lips and nodded.

The ambassador bobbed his head like a balloon. Made sense, Connie thought, he was full of hot air.

Her hopes withering, she turned her attention to Nick Atwell. She hated judging people on first meeting. Weighing how she might use them was totally distasteful. But years of watching her mother plead and beg from one level of government to the next had taught Connie plenty. She'd use any means and anyone to save her father. Nick had said he was sorry about her father. Just that. Simple, direct, and she was sure of it, sincere. That left her three options: flirt, beg, or charge.

She charged. Delicately. "Why are the British still here unless they feel they can make a difference?"

Nick raised his chin slightly as if sniffing the wind. At a nod from the ambassador, he spoke, steepling his fingers under his chin. "Why don't the British do something? Well. I have to admit I've been mildly curious about that myself from time to time."

The red rose up Whitcraft's cheeks until he looked like a beet in a bow tie.

"I'm sure the ambassador never entertains such doubts," Connie said, shamelessly buttering up the older man.

"Ah, no, heh heh," Whitcraft said. "I'm sure we've done all we could. You must excuse Nick here, he's our resident, ah . . ."

"Renegade?" Nick offered.

"Oh, Nick, certainly not. Don't be so hard on yourself," the ambassador blustered. "He's what you American's might call a crack-up."

"A cutup is the term, I believe," Nick corrected mildly.

"Uh, yes."

Connie fought a grin and lost. He was darling and undeniably attractive. She had to remind herself feckless charmers did her cause no good.

Nevertheless, a tiny twinge of gratitude pinged in her heart. Some people chose their words carefully because they cared very much about what they said. Diplomats, she'd found, were more likely to choose the path of least persistence, saying anything to get a thorny problem like hers with her father off their desks.

But Nick Atwell cared. She hadn't imagined that. The ambassador's quick frown and the subtle shake of his head told her as much.

Before she could appeal to Nick for help, he touched the knot in his tie, cleared his throat, and proceeded to spout the party line. For some reason, that bothered her more than all the ambassador's claptrap.

"As you know, the British government has publicly deplored the taking of hostages. Unfortunately, we can push only so much."

"You call demanding justice *pushing*?" Connie leaned across the space separating their chairs and laid her hand on his arm. "Mr. Atwell, if it were your father in prison, would you push *only so much*? Wouldn't you *do* something?"

He didn't meet her eyes this time, poking his handkerchief a bit deeper into his breast pocket. An expression darkened his features and his blue eyes took on a swift hard glint as he glanced at the ambassador. Connie could have sworn it was a silent accusation. In seconds it vanished.

"I realize this greatly upsets you," Nick said, turning back to her, covering her hand with his.

She coolly withdrew it. She would have sworn that was sincere, too, if she hadn't known the routine so well. Change the subject, turn the focus on her and not her father's release, call in underlings and foist her off on them. From what the ambassador had said, in his presence no less, one couldn't get more underling than Nick Atwell. Connie would have felt sorry for him if she'd had any sorrow to spare.

She rested her forehead on her fingertips. "I should have waited and not come straight here after the flight from Singapore. It's just that I was so anxious to be back in Lampura, to be this close to my father. And now . . ."

Her throat constricted and her eyes misted over. Damn these emotions, she couldn't afford to be written off as hysterical. "Excuse me."

"Certainly."

Before she could reach for her purse, Nick handed her the red silk handkerchief. She daubed at her eyes, inhaling a scent curiously like shoe polish. "Thank you."

"Of course."

She got up and walked to the window. "The aroma of these flowers, this heat has brought back such memories. I haven't been back since I was sixteen. Since they arrested him . . ."

She looked out over the jungle foliage; huge green fronds made up the forest as well as the roofs of most of the houses in Lampura City. Chalk-white walls of apartment blocks pocked with bullet holes lined the dusty road known in all seriousness as the Avenue de Charles de Gaulle. At the opposite end of the street, a thousand yards away, stood the gleaming facade of the capitol—this week in the hands of the government.

"My father has spent ten years in prison for no offense anyone will name. My mother fought ceaselessly for his release—and to give me a normal life. The effort killed her, this last spring."

Connie did her best not to cringe at the automatic condolences offered by the ambassador. She found herself waiting for Nick Atwell to say something.

When he didn't, she spoke to cover her disappointment.

"I realize this is no way to accomplish anything, making demands, raising my voice."

"And a delightful voice it is," the ambassador said in a pathetic attempt at charm.

"Perhaps you'd be so kind as to give me an appointment later in the week?" Connie gambled that the ambassador would jump at the chance to better prepare himself.

As it was, he hemmed and hawed until Nick stepped up behind her, just touching the back of her arm with his fingertips. Startling shivers of warmth ran along her skin.

"Miss Hennessy, perhaps you could tell me more. Say, in my office?"

Her shoulders sagged and she glanced over the treetops. Not even the promise of an appointment. They really wanted to get rid of her. Nick was the sacrificial assistant assigned the task.

"Or perhaps we could try the bar at your hotel?" he said. "I'd be honored to buy you a drink."

Whitcraft nodded vigorously, so eager to get her out of his office, one would have thought she was a ticking bomb. "Yes, Nick, you do that. Nick knows every bar in town."

Defeated for the time being, Connie nodded. No matter how many times she'd seen it happen to her mother, she never ceased to feel the sting of humiliation and resentment. The humiliation she would put up with to save her father; the resentment she reserved for the people who'd taken him hostage, forcing her into a role she hated.

"It's a bit early for a drink," she demurred as Nick led her through the door.

"Never too early for me," he laughed easily. "Do you feel up to the stairs?"

Her legs shook and she felt dizzy in the heat. "I'll be fine."

"You seem like a very strong woman."

"Not really." She smiled, used to these comments on her courage. She wasn't brave. She fought because she had to. Because she'd promised her mother she wouldn't give up. Because she was as far from brave or courageous or dutiful as a daughter could be. "I love my father. That's all."

Until she got him free, she loved no one and nothing else. But Nick was right, she could use a bracing drink.

Nick escorted her to the Imperial Hotel. Flowering hibiscus plants in terra-cotta pots flanked the door. A half dozen men lounged at sidewalk tables, playing the local form of checkers. Nick noted two or three government spies among them, two undercover rebels and George Cunningham from the embassy. George lifted a glass Nick's way with a look on his face that said, "That was fast."

A flash of shame cut through him. Sometimes being good at one's job wasn't something to be proud of. Nick escorted Connie to a private table.

"I can't see a thing," she declared.

"The eyes adjust."

She sank into a cane-backed chair in a dimly lit alcove. "Do the muscles? Or the pores? I get exhausted just breathing the air."

"A bit like walking underwater, isn't it? The rains should arrive in a couple of weeks."

"To think I loved this place when I was sixteen."

Nick studied the woman she'd become. She'd recovered beautifully in Whitcraft's office, then wished a very civilized good day to the staff as they'd walked out the door. But Nick, with his hand on her back, had felt her tremble.

It excited him, that sense of her body beneath her filmy clothes, her heated skin beneath his fingertips. He'd stuck his hands firmly in his pockets after they'd turned the first corner, ruing the day she'd appeared in his life, all of one hour ago.

He hailed the waiter and ordered a local fruit drink for her, a gin and tonic for himself.

The woman needed help, a shoulder to lean on. Unfortunately for him, she was too intelligent to accept excuses, platitudes, or any of the other rigmarole in the embassy's arsenal. And why should she? She had a cause worth fighting for.

Easy, Nick told himself. He wasn't here to get involved.

His unspoken assignment was clear: get her out of Whitcraft's hair, brush her off. It galled him that this gallant, beautiful, loyal daughter of a brave and wrongfully imprisoned man should be turned over to a stalled, once-promising diplomat to be shuffled off the premises.

Nick tasted the bitterness of a curse on his tongue and made a mental note to dig out the Hennessy file when he got back to the office. His hand froze in midair as he lifted the gin and tonic to his lips. For the first time in months he actually looked forward to going to the office. *Let that be a warning, old boy. A woman like Connie Hennessy could give a man a reason for living.*

He gave her a wink and decided to settle for her company and the pleased, startled look on her face. She was beautiful. And they had important things to talk about. "Tell me about him."

She thought a moment, smoothing droplets of moisture down the surface of her glass. In that instant, she was far, far away. "I've told this to so many people—"

"If you don't care to—"

"How can I expect people to help me if I don't tell them?"

Not that he'd made any promises. He could tell from the way her smile came and went that she was aware of that. He felt like a complete scoundrel.

He looked like the complete gentleman, Connie thought, so typically English. Cool, collected, reserved. Handsome in a careless way. He had wide shoulders that guaranteed jackets hung well, a neck long enough not to appear strangled by a collar and tie, and a trim waist from which faintly pleated slacks draped in subtle folds. He'd look good anywhere, fit in anywhere, and succeed at just about anything without undue effort. He'd certainly hustled her out of Whitcraft's office in record time.

Which left her with the nagging question of what a man of such apparent promise was doing in this remote corner of the globe. And why, as tired as she was, as disappointed, as oppressed by the heat, did she feel these inexplicable shivers of desire trembling beneath her skin?

Must be the turbulent emotions surrounding her return, she thought. Or the punch. *Koa-pora*, locally brewed, had an alcoholic content that by comparison reduced the gin in Nick's gin and tonic to soda pop.

He waited patiently for her to speak. For one drawn-out moment, she forgot the oft-repeated words. For one intriguing moment, she noticed nothing but the man across from her, his blue eyes and narrow mouth, the hard-won patience overlaying an urgency he didn't want her to see.

Was that because he wanted to help her or have her?

In the intimately dim light and slow-moving sultry air, the idea of being alone with him, of forgetting anything more urgent than passion, of giving herself over to something as basic as this man's touch, was darn near as seductive as her drink.

Connie shook her head and braced herself with another sip of punch. Sternly, she reminded herself she couldn't be seduced by someone listening. Not even this man and his intense, almost passionate concentration on everything she said.

No more sympathy without results, that was her motto. She didn't care if he cared, only that he give her help.

But he'd have to *care* to *help*, she thought.

She took a deep breath and resolved to make him care very, very much.

Two

"The country was in chaos," Connie began. "One day some soldiers hustled my father into a car and took him away. We suspected he was in the prison beneath the capitol building, but no one would let us see him. My mother and I were flown out of the country for our own safety.

"When the rebels seized Lampura City, they held him while waiting for American aid. It never materialized. When they refused to release him without the money, the Americans declared they wouldn't pay anything that smacked of ransom. Then the rebels made a videotape. On it Father declared he was fine and supported their cause completely."

"Coerced, I'm sure."

"So am I." Connie wished she could dismiss Nick's careful concern. As it was, every time he gave her that understanding, supportive look, she wanted to throw herself in his arms and sob. She sipped her drink. He finished his.

"Anyway," she continued, "when the government forces reclaimed the capitol, they accused father of collaborating with the rebels."

"Catch-22."

"Both sides have used him as a pawn and—" She swirled a piece of fruit around the rim of her glass.

"And?" Nick said no more, signaling the bartender with his empty glass.

"Every time the capitol changes hands, we have to—I have to wonder what will happen to him. If this side will release him. Or execute him. He can't stay in there forever."

Connie recognized real tenderness in Nick's gaze. She rubbed her forehead. "I'm so tired of overtures and embargoes and politicians' promises. No offense."

"None taken."

"You shrug this off very well."

He looked genuinely hurt.

Connie felt genuinely guilty.

"I'm listening, aren't I?" He reached across the table and gripped her hand.

She liked that. She shouldn't. "But will you *help* me?"

"How can I? The United Nations, the Red Cross, Amnesty International, they've all had a go at it."

She lowered her voice. "I wondered if an escape could be arranged somehow."

"From the rebel's bastion in the mountains? I'm a diplomat, not a magician. You'd need David Copperfield for that." He lifted his second drink off the tray as soon as the waiter arrived with it. "Thank you, Soo."

Connie reached across the table and touched his fingers as they curled around the glass, feeling the breadth and bony strength of the man's hand. "I don't blame you, Nick."

"Just all those diplomats and politicians."

"You said earlier that the embassy might do something for a change."

Ah, she was quick, Nick thought. Also compelling, fierce, intelligent, and wounded. With reason. Nick's heart went out to her. He brought it right back, firmly tucking it under his handkerchief where it belonged. "I hope it's some consolation to you that the rest of the world knows of his plight. Everyone admires the courage—"

"Oh, he's a hero all right. He'd go back to being a regular man in a minute."

"Yes, I'm sure he would." Nick took a long swallow of his drink. As usual, it did no good. At his direction, Soo made Nick's drinks ninety-nine percent tonic, nevertheless he felt the burn of gin all the way down his throat. The heat settled below his stomach.

Suddenly she smiled, lighting up this corner of the Imperial's bar. "I feel like a broken record."

"You don't look like one."

"You're better at flattery than Whitcraft."

"My ego would have been irreparably damaged if you'd said anything less. Would you mind terribly if I said you were something of a diplomat yourself?"

"Is that what I'm turning into?"

He grinned. "I may go further than I'd planned and say you have a lovely smile."

"Do you plan everything you're going to say?"

"Not often enough. It's gotten me in trouble on more than one occasion."

"Is that why they saddled you with me back at the embassy? Punishment?"

For a split second he couldn't keep the shock off his face. "You are a quick one."

"Will you help me?"

As to-the-point as the tip of a fencing foil, Nick thought. And as dangerous as only a woman in trouble could be.

The touch of her buffed nails on his wrist sent sparks up his veins like satellite signals, a code any man could decipher. Her voice was breathy, like a low wind rustling through a garden at night, reminding him of old dreams.

"Nick. I thought I detected a desire in you, a willingness to get involved."

Desire? Involvement? The speech he should have

delivered an hour ago came out in a rush. "Miss Hennessy, the embassy would love to help you under the proper circumstances, but surely you must see this is not our area."

"Save it, Nick. I've heard this part."

He admired the way she kept the bitterness out of her voice. Now if only she'd keep the hope out of her eyes. He had the unnerving sensation that she saw right through him. Thankfully, Soo was paying attention and brought over a third gin-and-mostly-tonic without being asked.

"Another punch?" Nick offered.

"No, thank you," she said.

"I forget myself. We should have begun with this." Nick raised his glass. "To Constance. An apt name for a daughter of such dedication."

"Thank you."

"I'm sure your father knows something of what you're doing for him. A man would be damned proud to have that kind of love in his corner." He certainly would.

Tears came to her eyes and she looked away. "I hope so."

Nick downed the third drink faster than the first two. Her gaze flickered toward the table, then away. People often counted the glasses that accumulated around Nick. No reason why it should embarrass him now. He hoisted his glass and spoke a little louder. "To Constance *and* Hennessy, a damn fine cognac. Wish they carried it here."

She glanced again at the glass wall being erected between them. Another tactful hint.

Connie collected her purse, her fingers clutching the patent leather until it dented. "You'll have to excuse me, I'm wiped out by the travel."

"As you wish," Nick replied equably. Let her dismiss him. Wouldn't do to give the woman the wrong impression.

"If you can't help me, why are you here?" She

asked so quietly it took him a moment to stop studying her softly rounded shoulders, those downcast eyes which were now fastened on him. Eyes as green as the sea surrounding them.

"In Lampura?" he asked disingenuously. "Or why am I here having a drink with a beautiful woman? I believe the latter is self-explanatory."

"The former," she asked, holding his gaze.

The *tenacious*, beautiful, gallant, loyal daughter . . . , he repeated to himself.

He jabbed the lacquered table with his finger. "I'm here because I got posted to tropically blessed Lampura, glittering island nation or Indian Ocean land mass, depending on whose atlas you believe. And *that*, Miss Hennessy, was because they didn't trust me anywhere else."

"That's a little blunt."

"But true."

"And you're the man they gave me to."

He chose to ignore the insult. "Wouldn't I be lucky if that were the case?"

"I meant—"

"I know what you meant. You're stuck with me."

"I'm going to save my father, Nick."

"Just don't take any foolish risks."

"I'll take whatever risks are necessary. Wouldn't you? If this were *your* father—"

"The reinstated government have clamped down so hard on the populace that the rebels are gaining favor again. No one is who they pretend to be, and absolutely no one can be trusted. Do you speak the local dialect?"

"No. We were here only six months."

"Then you don't have many options." And he wasn't offering any. *Be a cad, Atwell. Leave the woman to her own devices*. Which, in the best of times would bring her nothing but grief, in the worst of times they might get her killed.

She rose. "Thank you for the drink. I'm sorry I

wasted your time." She marched toward the archway leading into the main hotel.

Nick trailed after. Thanks to his long strides, he gained on her without appearing to hurry. As soon as they passed the front desk and turned into the corridor, he gripped her wrist, spinning her toward him. "You're not to hop in some Jeep and drive off into the mountains to see the rebels, understand? This isn't an adventure film."

"So what do I do? Throw myself on your mercy?"

He was almost flattered, until he realized she meant the embassy. "If you blunder into trouble of your own making, you'll get little help there."

"What about here?" She touched his chest.

He couldn't answer. He'd heard her out, warned her off, downed what she might have assumed was six fingers of gin, and the woman still wouldn't let him off the hook. Neither would his conscience. Why did he have to feel so damned responsible for people he couldn't help?

Connie knew he hadn't answered her question. She wanted to know why he felt it necessary to bring her here, to pay such close attention to everything she said or did, to drink gin like it was going out of style and draw attention to that fact, to chase her to the elevator for one more word.

Maybe she had her answer. Nick Atwell wanted to help her whether he knew it or not.

Connie slung her purse strap over her shoulder and got up on her tiptoes. She took his face in her hands and kissed him on the mouth. Let him blame *that* on the koa-pora. "Thank you for helping me."

"I don't see how I ever gave you that idea—"

"Because you're a better man than you like to think, Mr. Atwell."

"Not if you knew what I was thinking right now." When she would have set her heels back on solid ground, he caught her chin between his thumb and forefinger and lifted her mouth to his. His lips skimmed hers until they both trembled for more.

She felt starved, empty, as if the floor had swayed out from underneath her feet, as if the plane that brought her here hadn't quite landed, as if the island were a ship tossing on the ocean, rocking her toward him.

His hands rested lightly on the flare of her hips. Her mouth remained raised to his. Her breasts brushed his suit coat. His second sweeping kiss tasted tangy. In moments the taste grew stronger, as if she'd drunk from his glass instead of the velvety tip of his tongue.

Her eyes flew open and she stepped back, swaying on her high heels. "Excuse me!"

He held her waist, steadying her.

"It must be the heat." She knew her flushed cheeks would back up that white lie. "And the drinks."

"Must be."

She smiled a sickly smile. No wonder this man was a diplomat. Completely unruffled, he suavely pretended women threw themselves at him every day. Maybe they did. "I hope you don't think—"

A small shake of his head. "Not at all."

"I wouldn't— Not just to get you to—"

"I understand."

"It's just, you seemed to care." And getting him to care had seemed like such a good idea at the time, Connie thought.

"I'm sorry if I gave you the wrong impression."

"My mistake." Shame colored her cheeks. "The koa-pora."

"Yes, indeed."

They let the lie stand. Nick doubted she'd be dissuaded for long. He hoped not. She had something worth fighting for, someone, a rare and precious thing.

She walked a straight line down the black and

white parquet floor to the lone elevator. Nick watched her go, telling himself with her every step that he couldn't very well run after her. He'd already blundered by kissing her.

He caught up to her by the elevator. "Miss Hennessy, I keep my ear to the ground and every now and then I pick up some tidbit that might be useful."

She turned to him, her dignity back in place, the shame he'd put in her eyes ruthlessly mastered. "I didn't come for tidbits, thank you all the same."

"I'll see what I can put together. In a week or so I might have a few names for you, a pass—"

"Three days."

He grinned, and a weight he hadn't realized was there lifted off his chest. "Done."

They shook hands, the warmth of hers tempting him to press a little tighter. She gave no indication it mattered either way. The kiss could have happened in another lifetime, one as distant as the date on which this elevator had been installed.

An attendant folded open the ornate metal cage. Connie stepped in, and the contraption rose with a squeak and bray of cables. Nick wouldn't have entered that thing on a bet.

"Don't forget to check the desk for messages," he called after her, craning his neck to see up the shaft. Shoving his hands in his pockets, he backed toward the front desk and the bar beyond.

When Nick's parting words came back to Connie after she showered, she called the front desk. A message was there for her. She asked for it to be sent up, along with some bottled water, then she sank down on the bed, watching the fan blades spinning diagonal shadows around the ceiling, a black and white kaleidoscope spinning, spinning, and every design the same.

The knock at the door interrupted the deepest

sleep she'd had in days. Connie jumped up, waited for her head to stop whirling, and opened the door.

A short man the color of hickory nuts handed her a white note, folded once and printed on embassy stationery. It was an invitation to a ball the following evening. Loopy handwriting at the bottom, hastily scrawled, read:

> *Can't promise much. Will be a working dinner for me. Maybe some people of interest to you. Please come, Nick.*

A man of promise who made no promises, Connie thought, astonished at how the handwriting brought him back, more daring than sensible, chafing at invisible bonds.

She sympathized, forced as she was to live a double life of globe-trotting and public petitioning when all she wanted was peace and quiet—and her father back again.

What kind of double life did Nick Atwell lead? Could she trust him? Or anyone? Did she have a choice?

"Maybe you're reading way too much into this, kiddo," she muttered to herself. It wasn't hard when his smile stayed with her, the puzzling dichotomy between his easy manner and intense listening.

She scanned the note once more. Not even a salutation. Surprisingly careless about social amenities for a diplomat, she thought. Flipping over the heavy paper, she noted how carefully he'd written her name.

"They knew whose box to put it in with just 'Connie' on it?" Her voice echoed in the underfurnished room. She had the eerie feeling she was the only guest in the entire hotel. After all, her father's imprisonment was Lampura's single claim to fame. That and civil insurrections kept most tourists at bay.

An idea occurred to her. If she made contact with the government, got in to speak with the Premier-for-Life, she might hint at increased tourism in exchange for her father's release. The good press and goodwill—

Saving her father was *her* responsibility. She couldn't rely on well-meaning junior diplomats. And yet, visions of Nick Atwell intruded. She itched to ask him what *he* would do.

"He wants to help," she murmured, as if saying it aloud would make it true. She decided to accept the invitation.

"There will be other diplomats there," she explained aloud, opening her suitcases. "Effective ones. Ones who have better standing with the Foreign Office than dear, diffident Nick Atwell."

Who kissed like a warm lagoon.

"You kissed him first."

He was tipsy.

"What's *your* excuse?" she asked herself firmly. Punch? Jet lag?

Connie looked in dismay at her wrinkled wardrobe. What did one wear to an embassy ball in the tropics, anyway?

Not much, from the look of it. The men were in tuxes and the women were native or nonexistent. That meant sarongs wildly splashed with color, black hair to their waists, and sandals. Connie wore resuscitated chiffon, two layers of wafting material just begging to wrinkle and an underslip of basic black silk. Although the dress was simple and short, she felt like an overdressed partygoer.

It didn't help that twenty people, eager for a new face, turned as one when she entered. Where had she put that invitation? Come to think of it, where the dickens was Nick Atwell?

The man she'd pinned a few unrealistic hopes on

held up the bar in the far corner, trading chitchat with a portly man in a tux. The portly man nodded her way. Nick downed a drink and spun slowly around on his stool.

"Connie," he shouted over the hubbub, glass aloft. "What are you having, darling?"

She smiled stiffly. Ambassador Whitcraft bustled over, replacing his disapproving frown at Nick's behavior with a sympathetic smile for Connie.

"My dear. Welcome. Do come in, come in."

Connie felt her hand squished between the ambassador's sweaty palms.

"Let me introduce you around," Whitcraft rumbled.

She made her way through the small groups of shiny faces, trying her best to remember names, titles, possible future usefulness, and that indefinable sense of whether a person could be trusted. Not a one of them set off alarm bells like Nick Atwell.

"Most of us are staff, but there are a few journalist types about," Whitcraft stated, "covering the impending revolution and all that. Charles here, he's one of us. And Jackson. And Cunningham. Perhaps you've met."

Connie remembered George Cunningham, though she couldn't say why. He had a quiet, composed way of standing back and watching a person, a way of blending into walls while smiling and shaking one's hand.

"Good to see you again," he said. "I trust the weather isn't too hot."

"Not at all."

"I see our Nick's taken it on himself to be a one-man welcoming committee," Jackson joined in.

For a moment Connie felt slightly seasick at the idea that word of their kiss might have gotten around. In a closed society like this, secrets weren't secrets long.

"Don't mind Nick," someone said. "He prefers the bar to us."

"I've noticed he enjoys a good drink," she replied evenly.

"Good, bad, indifferent, never matters to Nick."

"Never drinks in his office though," Whitcraft added in his defense.

Jackson concurred. "Everyone needs his oasis—although in Nick's case, the oasis is the one dry spot and everything else is a sea of booze."

Male laughter sounded through the room.

Connie caught another glimpse of Nick and wondered if this afternoon's connection had been nothing but a reflection of her own longing for someone to help her fight, to combat the intense loneliness of being so far from home with no one on her side. She steadied herself—desires like that had led to Paul. She wouldn't make that mistake again.

At the bar Nick engaged the native bartender in desultory conversation while building a pyramid of his empties. The first row was three glasses wide, the second two-thirds built.

"I'd better say hello to the man who invited me," Connie said to George.

"Mm, better than having him make a scene."

"Would he?"

George shrugged. "He might call across the room that you're the most beautiful thing to happen to Lampura since the sunrise. A fiery-haired goddess of cinnamon trees, wise and enduring, with eyes from the sea. That sort of thing."

Connie flushed three shades of sunrise. "He didn't say that."

"To everyone who's approached the bar. It's practically a mantra."

"Good Lord. I'll talk to him."

"Just don't forget us," George said, smiling weakly.

"I won't."

Connie nodded to three undersecretaries in a row before she reached the one she'd come to see. "This is your idea of a working evening?"

With her standing and his right hip cocked on a stool, Nick and Connie were nose to nose. That gave him a heart-stopping view of her green eyes, threaded with gold and earthy brown. Devoid of illusions.

"Evening, Miss Hennessy. Yes, this is my work. I socialize without being a socialist. Commune without being a communist. Come to the party and follow the party line."

"You're drunk."

"And you're disgusted with me. About time." He turned back to his pyramid.

"Did you invite me so I could see this?"

He grinned without looking up. "I know your father is your main concern, Connie. Your only concern. But if you ever require a little rest and recreation while in our sunny country, if you'd like some fun—"

"Fun."

"Don't leap at the offer. I'll be here all evening."

"And late into the night from the looks of it."

"You're far from tactful."

"I don't have time. I came here to—"

He held up his hand, a cocktail umbrella waggling between his fingers. "I know why you're here."

"If you don't want to help, say so."

"I thought I had."

"All right, then."

After a silent moment spent staring deeply into the swirling brown of his whiskey glass, Nick spun around, managing to look surprised. "You still here?"

"You offered me a hearing today. A sympathetic ear."

"Like van Gogh but without the mess." He tugged on his lobe.

She made a face.

He hoped he wouldn't fall head over heels in love with a woman because she made funny faces. If he couldn't shoo her away soon, he just might. Or should he say, he already had? Since that unfortunate circumstance seemed to be the case, he wondered what his next move should be.

She folded her arms and smiled knowingly. "You're not as drunk as you pretend."

"Let's not trade insults, please."

"I saw you thinking this out. You're only pretending to be drunk!"

He stood and took her elbow in his hand. Twisting toward the bar, he grabbed his unfinished drink, clutched a second glass with his thumb, and escorted her quickly across the room and out the long veranda doors. "Right-o. Out we go."

Three

They emerged onto a balcony overlooking Lampura City. Dots of electric light glittered fitfully at their feet, strings of illumination outlining the city in neat rows. Empty thoroughfares sloped toward the glimmering moonglow of the Indian Ocean, then ended abruptly. Streetlights, swallowed by the sea, were extinguished like candles but without the sizzle.

"What was that all about?" Connie demanded, removing her arm from Nick's grip.

"Haven't you ever been swept off your feet?"

"That was more like a bum's rush!"

Nick wished she wouldn't stand with her arms folded like that. The chiffon outlined her breasts, small but pert. Mouth-size. He swallowed hard, his Adam's apple barely clearing his black tie. "Your drink."

She grimaced when he took his thumb out of it.

"Alcohol will kill the germs," he added helpfully.

"The ways it kills memories? Why did you join the Foreign Legion and come to this desolate spot?"

"For one thing, it's the Foreign Office. For two, they consider me too unreliable for anything else, as I believe I told you."

"And told me and told me. You're trying to throw me off, aren't you, Nigel?"

"Nick!" An absolute panic shot through him at the idea that she'd forgotten his name.

She smiled like the Mona Lisa. "Okay. Nick."

He tugged on his collar and looked out over the city. "Gave myself away, did I?"

"For a second. Now tell me about it."

It. His long-lost career. "I joined the Diplomatic Service with visions of world peace, common sense, and negotiation dancing in my head. Make love not war, that's my motto." Disheveled but debonair, he leaned an elbow on the railing and smiled.

"You're a flirt too."

His smile disappeared. "Not a naive one. And not so idealistic as I once was."

"Why not?"

He shrugged, turning his back to the view and waving his glass at the gathered guests inside. "I thought once I might make a difference. Like Raoul Wallenberg, the Swedish diplomat who saved so many Jews right under Hitler's nose. Or Terry Waite negotiating for the hostages in Lebanon. However, it was quickly brought home to me that our real business is maintaining the status quo." He looked at her a moment, aware he'd been rattling on.

She rekindled old fires. Whether it was the burning desire to change the world, or one messed-up speck on it, he didn't know. Maybe it was plain garden-variety desire. In which case, he'd dearly love to kiss her again. He bent forward.

"Is that why you drink?" she asked quietly.

"I don't envy the rebels once you get your teeth into them."

"I'm frankly surprised you haven't risen farther faster. You're so good at evading direct questions."

She dipped her finger into her glass and placed a bead of whiskey on her tongue. "Nobody trusts you. Why do I, I wonder?"

Nick drew himself up to his full height, one hand straying to his cummerbund. He took a slow deep breath, regaining his balance, like a tightrope walker suspended above flames of desire. "I have never given away secrets or betrayed a confidence," he stated forcefully. He lowered his voice. "I do, however, have this distressing tendency to speak my mind when I care strongly about something, especially injustice. Cardinal sin in this line of work."

"I can imagine."

"So there's this blot on my record. Unreliable, it says in my file. Right next to Indiscreet." He frowned at his empty glass. "You'd do well to stay away from me."

"Is that why you have your so-called drinking problem?"

For one dizzying second he couldn't lie to her, not even dissimulate. Oh, this was bad. He'd be pouring out his heart to her next. "I, uh, don't. Not really." He didn't expect her to believe it. No one else did. "To be honest, alcohol doesn't have much effect on me."

"So you pretend it does."

His heart did a flip in his chest. She actually believed him. "Thanks." He lifted his glass. "This round's on me."

She smiled and shook her head at his nonsense, letting her hip brush his as she took a place beside him at the rail. "Those are real whiskeys."

He shook his head almost sadly. "Yours is. Mine is half water."

"Still. Half of five drinks . . ."

"Could be ten. Alcohol has virtually no effect on me. Never has. Sometimes I wish it would. You see, Connie—"

She smiled when he used her name. He wished he hadn't done it precisely for that reason.

"—if I drink, others believe I'm drunk and then I can say anything I want. It's just good old Atwell at the well again, so to speak. It gives me a certain license."

"A liquor license," she said.

He laughed and lifted his glass to her. "Exactly."

She touched his arm. He tried not to quiver. Every corner of his brain was on alert—his body was even more so.

"Let me get this straight, Nick. It's more important to you to speak up about how you feel than to whitewash things." She clucked. "That would be a problem for a diplomat."

"Considering the fact it landed me here, I'd have to agree." He raised his glass. "To the island of Lampura, and a lovely, constant lady."

She raised hers to her lips, a thoughtful, troubled look on her face. "To a man with a problem—which doesn't happen to be drinking."

"I thought I explained that."

"You still have a problem."

"Which is?"

"Turning me down."

"I wasn't aware you'd made any improper suggestions." He trailed a finger along her sleeve, the skin inside it shivering from touch on chiffon. He felt goose bumps. He wondered what that did to her nipples. He knew what it did to his. "Who says I'd turn you down?"

"You want to help me. Maybe you don't feel capable."

He frowned at her dare and looked out over the city, more sober than he wanted to be. Trying to keep up with him had made her slightly drunk. He assumed that was the only reason she leaned toward him now, her eyes glowing with hope and starlight, her body coming nearer as she set one dainty hand on his chest, covering his rapidly beating heart, her face lifted to his.

"Goodness, look at the time!"

She pursed her lips in gentle reproof. "There are no clocks out here, Nick."

At least she got the name right. He lifted her wrist, turning it to read her bracelet watch. "Almost midnight."

"What happens then?"

He swallowed, a treacherous breeze carrying the scent of her over him like a dream that evaporated the moment one opened one's eyes. Dancers frozen in a slow dance, he held her wrist tucked against his chest. Her skin was pale and moon-white, her pulse thrumming beneath his thumb. The sultry night air spiraled around them.

He wanted her mouth to open under his, her lips to spread at his silent injunction. They did.

He didn't care who saw. He'd stopped counting how long they'd been out here and how many people might notice. He was drunk—that was his excuse—and she knew it wasn't true. Only she would understand how desperately he needed a woman to believe in him at last. "Connie."

"Kiss me again."

A rocket thudding into the side of the embassy couldn't have rocked him the way her throaty plea did. He clamped an arm around her back and let her feel, body to body, what a kiss between them could be, what promises it held.

"Ah, here you are."

They sprang apart, or would have if Nick hadn't clutched her close for one second more, an unmistakable fire in his eyes. "Not yet," he said on a breath for only her to hear.

Impolitic as it was at this point, Nick ignored Cunningham's soft cough and skimmed his mouth along Connie's cheekbone, lost in the shadows of her auburn hair. "Slap me," he whispered.

She hesitated. He pinched her bottom.

She jerked out of his arms as if stung and landed

a haymaker on his right cheek. The night rang with it.

So did Nick's ears. He rocked back on his heels and slowly lifted a hand to his face. "Why, Miss Hennessy. I didn't know you cared."

"Something going on out here?" Whitcraft huffed as he took another step onto the balcony. "George?"

Connie swept past them and disappeared into the ballroom.

"Just another revolution," Cunningham replied.

"Not another!"

"Minor skirmish," Nick winked, patting the ambassador on the arm. "War between the sexes, don't you know."

Nick left it to Cunningham to explain, heading back to his secure perch at the bar. His walk was unsteady, his smile forced. It wasn't until he caught sight of himself in the long mirror over the rows of bottles, that he recognized the outline of a bright red feminine hand imprinted on his right cheek.

"Lady troubles?" the bartender asked.

Nick surreptitiously scanned the room, overhearing gusts of derisive laughter as the balcony scene made the rounds. She was gone.

All right, he thought. He'd thrown Cunningham and Whitcraft safely off the track. But not Connie. She kept *him* off track. She got on his nerves and under his skin. She saw through him to the man he'd always wanted to be, to heroic fantasies he'd thought firmly crushed ages ago.

He was sick and tired of hiding behind a bottle so he could speak the truth. Who was Connie Hennessy to stir up these feelings anyway? What was she? The list grew so long he alphabetized it: bold, brave, dedicated, gallant, trustworthy, vulnerable, wounded. Sexy, he'd have to put that in there somewhere. What did it matter? He couldn't have her. Didn't deserve her. Not unless he helped her first.

"Can a man overcome his past?" he asked aloud.

The bartender reached for the bottle and began pouring him another shot. Nick put a hand over his glass too late; a sluice of whiskey dribbled down his cuff.

"I mean it, Soo. Can a man be redeemed by the love of a good woman?"

There. He could sneer at it. His hand stopped shaking, his heart stopped drumming, and the fire in his flesh subsided to a manageable level. Now if only his cheek would stop stinging.

He glanced in the mirror, turning his head. He was a marked man. No doubt about it.

"Whatever help I can offer would be strictly personal," he said. "If anything goes wrong, the embassy will disavow any involvement and leave us both twisting in the wind."

"And those are the people you work for," Connie said softly, her voice sending tiny rills of sensation to him through the phone wires.

Nick tapped a local coin against the corrugated tin wall of a bar in one of the ramshackle districts of the city. He would have called her from his apartment in the embassy, but there was never any telling if they tapped his phone. "They barely trust me to decipher codes."

Harry had sent him one today, a quote from *Nicholas Nickleby*: "I know the world and it knows me."

Connie didn't seem to care what the world thought. "I trust you," she said. "You do their dirty work?"

"Being expendable has made me indispensable."

"You're indispensable to me."

He leaned against the tin wall and it almost collapsed. This place was as shaky a premise as the one he was about to make. "I want to talk to you."

"About that kiss?"

"I want to help."

He expected a whoop of joy, a gushing thank you. Her long pause told him he didn't understand the woman at all.

In her hotel room Connie clamped a hand over her mouth to suppress a cry. She swallowed the lump in her throat, holding the receiver of the heavy black phone to her chest. A riot of vermilion flowers clambered up the balcony, flashes of color she knew she'd always associate with elation. "Thank you," she whispered, "thank you, you wonderful man."

Only the flowers heard.

"Are you there?"

"Yes, Nick, I'm here."

It was all she could manage. Gratitude, admiration, affection, a host of emotions battered her like storm-tossed waves, a whirlpool with Nick Atwell at its center. A misplaced but compelling desire to touch him overcame her, to cup his cheek in her palm, to run her fingers down the slope of his face, to kiss him, communicating beyond words what he meant to her at this moment.

"About that kiss," he began, as if reading her thoughts.

"I didn't kiss you so you'd help me, Nick. I'm not promising anything like that in exchange for getting my father out."

"Of course not."

Gentlemanly, too, Connie thought, but vowed to keep her tone as professional and disinterested as his. "I know this is my fight, Nick, but I do appreciate the help."

"On the contrary. You're not entirely alone in this. You don't have to be."

Not anymore, she thought. "Call me when you get results. And Nick? Thanks again."

"Sure thing."

He rang off, convinced he'd successfully kept his infatuation with her under wraps. He hadn't made any promises, hadn't gone out on any limbs he couldn't back down.

In the corner of the dark bar he flipped a coin. Tails she loved him, heads she knew better.

Heads. Good. One of them ought to.

Nick's phone rang two days later. He was in his office mulling over a tip a man in southern Lampura City had given him over two koa-poras and a pint of Guinness. The ringing jangled his stomach, but his head was clear.

"You would like to come to the capitol building, Mr. Atwell. Your lady friend has gone in, an hour since, but has yet to come out. One hour."

The line went dead.

Nick's throat was dry, his skin clammy. Every vile rumor he'd heard about the dungeons below the capitol came to mind. He stood, looking left, then right, as if deciding which way to walk around his desk. It was either that or vault it.

He traipsed down the staircase as if heading out for a stroll. At the embassy's large double doors, he tugged a blue silk handkerchief from his breast pocket, dislodged three sets of matchbooks from last night's excursions, and made a show of dusting his shoes.

The humidity suffocated him, the sun beat down. Sweat trickled inside his waistband, spreading like a stain up his shirt. He wouldn't think about what he'd do when he got to the capitol building, looming one thousand yards ahead. If Connie had been so foolish as to walk right into government headquarters . . . If the Premier held her now. . .

A sick feeling clawed at him as he climbed the steps of the capitol to the shade of the overhang above the massive pillars. A short, brutish man with a face like crinkled leather lifted a rifle across his chest, sluggishly snapping to attention.

"Nicholas Atwell, British Embassy. I believe Miss Hennessy is somewhere on the premises."

"American?" The man made a gesture with his gun in one hand, his other forming a womanly curve indicating shoulders, waist, hips. A leer revealed brownish teeth.

"Yes," Nick said, keeping an icy fury under control. "American woman."

"Go with him."

Nick saw no one. Then a man stepped out of the dim interior and motioned to him. Nick followed, concentrating on little things like the pattern in the tile, the intricately carved woodwork, the fact this building had cost one fourth of Lampura's national worth.

When he got to see the Premier-for-Life, he'd improvise. It couldn't be any worse than retrieving Connie from Whitcraft's office. He'd breeze in, address the man politely, benignly rip his throat out if he'd so much as laid a hand on her.

The guard marched Nick around the elaborately carved staircase to a concealed elevator door which opened soundlessly on a stainless steel interior.

"We go down."

Down to the soundproofed fortified basement where the torture chambers, euphemistically named interrogation rooms, sat waiting. The very thought of Connie there made Nick quake.

So did the elevators. He stepped on board, loosening his tie, focusing on the grinning guard. Fierce determination fired him. If Connie was in trouble, they wouldn't have let him walk right in like this. She might not even be here. The call could have been a ruse. *Or a trap.* If he disappeared, the embassy would suppose him dead drunk in a ditch somewhere.

Instead of just dead.

For some reason the idea didn't bother him half as much as the thought of any harm coming to Connie Hennessy.

The guard studied him with beady eyes. He tipped his cupped hand toward his mouth. "Drink? You like, yes?"

Appalled but not surprised that this man might have drunk with him somewhere, Nick thrust a hand into his pocket and came out with a local bank note, large denomination. "Here. Buy yourself a round. Buy your regiment a round."

The man nodded mournfully. "Half them desert to the rebels in the hills."

"Too bad," Nick replied automatically, careful not to reveal any political preference.

The guard stood at attention as the elevator thudded to a silent halt. The doors opened with a whisper uncannily similar to the sound a .45 made when fired with a silencer.

The guard lowered his gun until the tip prodded Nick's chest. "Out."

Nick stepped into an antiseptically tiled hallway lit with a string of bare bulbs. The muzzle beneath his chin backed him up. "I demand to see Miss Hennessy." The echo of his firm voice mocked him up and down the empty hall. "Now."

The guard laughed. "So go, English."

"Nick?" Connie's voice sounded from down the hallway, thin, frail, ghostly.

Nick whirled. Like a nightmare, a dozen studded metal doors showed their gray faces to him. He noticed one ajar and gently pushed it open. "Connie?"

She sat on a bench which was suspended from the wall by two chains. She blinked up at him, as if the glaring bulb mounted to the ceiling in a cage of wire were too bright.

"Are you all right?" He wanted to go down on one knee and hold her to him. He couldn't move.

She wore a chic two-piece suit, gold buttons glittering on both sides of the lapels, the kind a woman wore to meet a president. The soft pink fabric warmed a room of white enamel. She crossed her ankles demurely, her hands folded in her lap—not tight, not loose. There was no fear in her at all. And no life in her eyes.

"Connie."

"Four years he spent in here."

Nick made his legs move. His touch on her arm barely registered. Her voice was neither loud nor soft, not angry, not accepting.

"Where did the rebels take him, Nick?"

"The first time they seized the capitol they probably kept him right here."

"With no window?"

"Who knows?"

"And when the government seized the capitol after the second revolution?"

"The rebels took him to the mountains."

"Do you think it's better than here? Where he is?"

"How long have you been in this cell?" He grabbed her by the shoulders but couldn't snap that glazed look out of her eyes.

"The Premier said I could visit. See how clean and well kept it was."

"And you came down here of your own accord? Don't you realize they could have slammed that door on you at any time? Held you prisoner too?"

They still could. Catching himself in time, Nick shut up. She didn't need lectures. She needed out. If his taut nerves and dry mouth were any indication, so did he. "We're going home."

"I wish we could," she said softly, resting her head on his shoulder. "I want to go with you."

He got her down the hall and into the elevator. The guard slung his rifle strap over his shoulder and pushed the button. All the way to ground level, Nick envisioned using that strap to strangle the man.

"Nick?"

He realized he'd been squeezing the life out of Connie's hand. "Sorry."

The doors swished apart. Fifty steps. That's how far it was across the marble floor to the main door. It creaked when they opened it. Maybe that was the sound of Nick's nerves strained to the breaking point.

When they stepped into the open air, the heat washed over them in waves. Nick mopped his brow with his handkerchief.

"Take me to the hotel," Connie said, her voice so far away, he almost didn't recognize it.

Connie couldn't look at the vines climbing the stained wallpaper of her room without seeing white enameled brick. Did they hose down the cells, she wondered. The smell of disinfectant clung to her the way silenced screams clung to those walls.

"Darling."

Nick's voice penetrated. He sat on her bed, watching her.

"This is how big his cell was." Connie paced off eight steps. "As big as this square of matting at the foot of the bed."

"I saw."

She'd gone over it and over it, telling Nick everything, seesawing from despair to righteous anger. "I *had* to appeal to the Premier. I can't sit around doing nothing." She sighed. "Why am I taking this out on you? You're the only one who's even tried to help."

Nick patted the bed, but she was too tightly wound up to sit down yet.

"I may not have shown it at the time, but I was never happier to see anyone than I was to see you this afternoon."

"Same here." He toasted her with a sip of gin.

If the man hadn't literally saved her life, he was doing his best to save her sanity by letting her talk this out. "You're a good listener," she said softly.

Nick knew her story by heart now—and his reactions to it, particularly the outrage that curled in his stomach every time he pictured Connie in that cell. He poured her a glass of the gin he'd had sent to the room the moment they arrived. "Sip this. It'll relax you."

"Relax?" Her sharp retort rang in the room. She wrapped her arms around her waist and buried her hands in the bend of her elbows, keeping it in as best she could. "I was in the room my father was in. How many years, Nick? Four years in that place! Four years!"

Nick put his arm around her.

"I'm sorry, I shouldn't yell at you."

"Yell, hit, scream, whatever you need."

She looked up; at last he'd broken through the maze of awful images. "You made me slap you at the ball."

"You didn't have to do such a good job of it." He rubbed his cheek.

"Why?"

"So no one would take us seriously."

"That makes no sense."

Nick chucked her under the chin. "If anyone thought I was really in love, my reputation would be ruined. Normally my love affairs are brief, messy, and shallow as the lagoon. No one on this island is used to taking me seriously. It would be a terrible shock if they did."

"I do."

"Precisely what I'm afraid of."

Once again Connie knew he was putting her off, playing the rake for her sake. She was too frazzled to chase down the reasons why, so she played along, struggling to keep her mood as light as his. "You have a lot of them? These love affairs?"

"Recently? No. Too bored. Too tired."

He tipped her glass to her lips. She sipped. He watched her lick a droplet off her upper lip.

"Yes, well," he murmured. "If I got too serious

about you, the staff might wonder what old Atwell was up to, sneaking around Lampura, asking questions."

"Is that what you've been doing?"

"I'm sure they thought I was sneaking away for a rendezvous with you. Hope you don't mind."

On the contrary. She felt closer to Nick than anyone since her mother's death. He cared. He came through. What better qualities could a man possess?

She shivered, feeling suddenly cold and very alone. She put down her glass, rubbed her arms, and looked to him for silent permission. When he set his glass on the bedside table, she gingerly let her body slip in close to his for warmth. "Do you want to?"

"Want to what, love?"

"You keep calling me that."

"You need to be called that." He tucked her head under his chin.

"Did you want to sneak away for a rendezvous with me?"

"I think of nothing else."

"Liar," she teased weakly. "I can't cry. Why is that?"

"Shock probably."

"I don't want to forget."

"You think you ever could?"

She almost crumbled then, the sincerity of his question cutting through her. She held him tight.

"You need someone to tuck you in when the adrenaline wears off," he murmured, his breath stirring her hair.

She wanted to bury her face against his jacket. He smelled so good, his shirt permeated with the odors of Lampura, dark green fronds, smoky rooms in grass houses, heat, musk, Nick. She rubbed her nose back and forth against his neck, tickled by stubble. "You don't go in for close shaves, Mr. Atwell."

She felt his Adam's apple bob.

"I had as close a shave as I needed today."

She laughed, then stiffened, not wanting to see it again, to remember.

"I don't want you thinking of that," he ordered, lifting her chin.

"Nick." She clutched his waist, feeling his body tighten as she reached inside his jacket. "I won't forget today, whatever happens."

"Neither will I. I promise."

He looked deep in her eyes and Connie knew something important wasn't being said. A man who didn't make any promises just had.

"Will you put me to bed?" she asked.

He nodded, his expression unreadable, his eyes wary.

It didn't matter. Connie suddenly had enough courage for both of them. Marching into countless embassies and politician's offices had taught her to be brazen, to come right out and ask for what she wanted.

She wanted Nick, now. She wanted the comfort he offered. She desperately required the closeness. He claimed no thanks were necessary. But they were deserved.

However, brazenness was one thing, conveying her desires another. A life of upheaval hadn't given her a great deal of experience with men. Banishing all doubts, Connie lifted her arms and reached around to the buttons on the back of her blouse. As her breasts pressed flat to his chest, Nick's breathing deepened. So did hers.

"Going to bed is a good idea." She lowered her arms and undid the zipper on her skirt. The tiny teeth chattered as they spread, revealing the silk inside, the blushing pink.

Nick steadied her when she stepped out of her shoes and tilted precariously toward him. His jaw clenched until it ached. He'd keep one of them upright if it was the last thing he did.

Four

"Would you prefer if I stepped into the hall?" An element of hoarseness crept into Nick's voice.

Connie laughed as if that were a silly question. "I'll keep the slip on."

He stood there like a lamppost, glaring at the smudges on his shoes, the shadows on the bed-spread. Out of the corner of his eye he caught a sleepy smile on Connie's face.

"You look uncomfortable," she said. "Hot."

She curled an unpainted fingernail around his collar button. It popped free. She tugged on one end of his tie with one hand and slid the knot down with the other. "You've been so good to me, Nick."

He gulped.

"You've been brave, trustworthy, dependable."

"Wonderful qualities in a guide dog."

She popped more buttons, one, two, three, *tsk*ing as she went. The tick of her fingernails was no match for the pound of his heart—snare drums meeting kettle drums. He took a deep purposeful breath and willed himself to relax. His reaction to her wasn't anything he couldn't control. He closed his hands around her wrists. Her skin was softer than kid gloves, smoother than flannel. Her pulse skittered as badly as his as he ran his hand to the crook of her arm.

He ruthlessly reminded himself she didn't mean this. "You're in shock."

"You want me to lie down?"

"Yes. No."

"Which is it?"

"I'm sure you know."

"I think I do." She smiled a private smile and sat on the edge of the bed. Crossing her legs, she reached up under the hem of her slip to unclip a garter and roll her stocking down. "It feels so good to get these off," she sighed. "Maybe the slip too—"

"Keep the slip on." His voice boomed in the room.

The man had tried so hard to convince her he was worthless. She wanted to prove otherwise.

Standing, she pulled the spread to the foot of the bed and folded down the sheet. "You sound like you could use another drink."

"I'm fine."

"Then tuck me in."

She settled in with a wriggle of her hips. All Nick had to do was draw the sheet over her legs, across her knees, past her waist outlined in pink slip, and over the creamy lace of the cups that held her breasts. He drew it all the way to her chin. He planned to cap this daring feat of willpower with a chaste kiss on her forehead. Then she coiled her fingers around his wrist.

He sank onto the edge of the bed, his feet firmly on the floor. "Love. Darling."

"Yes?"

He frowned a mighty frown. It didn't do much good when her eyes were at half-mast. Movie publicists called those bedroom eyes. He didn't want to think about it. "You've had a bad shock."

"Give me a good one."

"I couldn't."

"You aren't gay, are you?"

"Certainly not."

"Married?"

"Never."

"Celibate?"

"Hardly. My application for sainthood was lost in the mail. At least I think it was, the Pope never wrote me back. Rude of him."

"Very funny. Why don't *you* relax?"

"I will when you're safely asleep."

That wasn't entirely true. Judging from the last few days, Nick probably wouldn't relax until this beautiful and daring woman was out of the country. Or when her next words ceased to be permanently inscribed on his fantasy life.

"And if I don't want to sleep?"

He tried to answer. Her voice, throaty and low, prevented him. Her hand on his thigh bolted him upright.

"I want to thank you, Nick."

"No thanks are necess—"

She put her fingertips over his lips. "I want you to hold me. Please. I need to trust somebody. You were there. You're the only one who can understand."

The vulnerability in her green eyes got to him. Her honesty, her courage, speared him. Like Saint Sebastian, he now knew what it felt like to be pierced by arrows. Only in his case, the arrows were from Cupid's quiver.

If she felt frightened, alone, Nick was cursed to do something about it. He didn't ask himself how he'd won that honor or how he'd ever earned her trust. He just knew he'd die before he'd willingly lose it.

He skimmed the lace of her bra. Her eyes fluttered closed and she breathed a thank you. The hard peak of her nipple nudged his palm.

He promised himself he'd stop in a minute, after

he ministered to her other breast. It amazed him what a man could do with one foot firmly on the floor—and how hard it was keeping it there. Her breasts flushed a satiny pink, pebbled and tender. A sheen of perspiration made a path between them. One of his hands slid effortlessly down her back to encompass the flare of her hip, the soft give of her derriere when he urged her closer.

Short of breath, hard as a rock, he managed to turn that into a brotherly hug. "Are you relaxed now?"

"I'm scared." It was true. Connie had never felt more vulnerable. And yet, she'd never been more willing to take an emotional risk. Astonishingly easy, really. No negotiating, no equivocating. Connie had a lifetime's experience asking for what she wanted. If she didn't always get it, she didn't give up trying. "Are *you* scared, Nick?"

"Nonsense. I seduce women who are in shock every day of the week."

She laughed, reassured. She touched him, feeling the reverberation of his heartbeat through his shirt. When she kissed the side of his neck, that heartbeat could have been heard in Ceylon.

He stopped her with a light kiss of his own. Stopping there was sheer hell. "I won't take advantage. You can trust me that far."

"I'd trust you to the ends of the earth."

"In case you hadn't noticed, that's exactly where we are."

"Joker. I believe in you, Nick, no matter what anyone says."

"You'd be wise not to."

The soberness in his voice made her pause. She nudged a pillow up behind her back and leaned against it to study him. Her fingers entwined with his on her sheet-covered thigh; he wasn't getting away that easily. "You marched me out of that building without a single false step."

"Improvisation and dumb luck. That was a very dangerous situation." Time for the lecture he hadn't had the heart to deliver earlier. "What you did was as smart as a sheep offering itself to the wolves. You're never to do that again. Understand?"

Her lashes kissed her cheeks as she looked contritely at her lap. "I promise."

"All right. I've heard you rented a Jeep."

"You have good contacts."

"I don't want you straying into rebel territory with it."

"How am I to know what's rebel territory and what isn't?"

"Good point."

"I can't stay in here waiting for shreds of information and old leads." She swung her free hand to indicate the hotel room, the wallpaper revealing its grime in the late afternoon sun. "I came here with a purpose, Nick. Nothing's going to stop me until I've exhausted every possibility."

Nick sighed. There it was again. The strength and determination she paraded as if everyone owned an equal supply. Connie was direct, honest. She didn't think like a sniper taking aim; a spy betraying the weak, the trusting; a hostage-taker. There'd been occasions when he'd had to. He knew how to protect her from that sort—or so he'd thought until this afternoon.

"You'll simply have to let me guide you." It was the only answer. "From now on, we go everywhere together."

"We do?"

"I know some villages where we can ask some questions. *We*, Connie. None of this Lone Ranger derring-do."

"Cross my heart, Tonto." She did just that, drawing a finger across the mound of her left breast.

Nick wondered what kind of fresh hell he was

volunteering for now. He could barely keep his hands off her today, what would he do with her in a Jeep in the jungle-covered mountains of Lampura? What *wouldn't* he do, was more like it.

"I'll be going, then."

She lifted their joined hands and splayed her fingers so his could slip out. "Go."

He meant to, as soon as he figured out how to stand up and walk out while politely camouflaging his erection.

"But answer me one question first," she said.

Nick snatched her skirt from the floor and held it in front of him, using the excuse to pick up every dainty piece of clothing she'd dropped as she undressed. "What is it?"

"*Are* you doing all this to seduce me?"

Keeping his back to her, he neatly folded the items into a pile on a musty easy chair. "You're to stay here the rest of this evening. I don't want you out of that bed."

"Yes, sir."

He didn't turn, not even for the witchy smile he imagined curving her lips.

"You haven't answered my question."

"I will tomorrow. Before then I have some phone calls to make." It sounded lame the minute he said it.

"And I have to wash my hair." She swung her legs out of bed and waltzed into the bathroom.

Nick knew shock had as many peaks and valleys as an aerial map of Lampura. He hadn't been prepared for this. The warped bathroom door swung partially open behind her. Oblivious, Connie stripped off her slip and turned on the shower. She wrapped a towel around her and leaned against the door jamb just in time to catch Nick folding the last of her clothes.

"I'm sorry, Nick."

"For what?" He sounded like a schoolboy whose voice had suddenly changed. He brought it back to its normal register. "For what?"

"For making this so hard on you."

If she only knew.

"I was a little overwhelmed today."

He knew the feeling.

The shower's roar changed as she stepped into it. Water pounded the tin walls like a monsoon, pattering against the plastic curtain, pummeling her naked body. Picturing it, Nick groaned and sank onto the chair, right on top of her skirt and blouse.

The lady was high on adrenaline and fear, and he wasn't far from the same feelings. Ever since this afternoon he'd wanted to crush her in his arms, assuring himself she was safe with him.

She needed to be saved *from* him.

She wanted the strong resolute hero she imagined him to be. He couldn't blame her for being fooled. His actions had surprised even him.

Not that he hadn't faced danger before. Questioning government spies, drinking with paranoid rebels who wore bandoliers of extra bullets, as if one into the brain wouldn't do the job perfectly adequately. If either side had ever suspected him of favoring the other, he'd have been dead long ago.

He'd never felt so alive. Or like such a fraud. Connie thought he cared about her father. He only cared about her.

He listened to the rattling water. Mist penetrated the slit in the curtain. He decided to stay a bit longer. She might pass out. She might need him.

She'd told him as much. After what she'd been through, he could easily take advantage. And take and take. He pictured the fan swirling lazily overhead while she circled her hips on his. She'd look down at him.

And he'd look down at himself ever after for deceiving a woman in distress. Noble of him. "Who died and made you Saint George?" he muttered.

He was no hero. He was crazy about the woman, the best of all motives for going in the other room and taking her in his arms. He'd been frankly scared out of his wits when he got that phone call and learned she was in the depths of the capitol building. All he wanted was to touch her, to assure himself she was here and safe. To keep her that way until he could get her off this island.

Unfortunately, she wouldn't go without her father. Securing Bill Hennessy's release would be darn near impossible. Just the same, he'd been turning over possibilities in his mind since he'd met her.

So take a little of what she's offering, his libido urged.

Not bloody likely. Despite all his guff about disreputable conduct, he knew he'd never sink that low. Even antiheroes had their standards.

Connie soaped her hair and soaped it again. She spread suds over her entire body. Ever since the cell she'd felt dirty, restless. She told herself it was fear, but a skin-abrading washcloth couldn't remove the tingling feverish expectancy just below her skin. That was Nick.

"Oh, Connie," she sighed. From Mata Hari to femme fatale in one day wasn't like her at all.

"He didn't do anything," she sternly reminded her image in the fogged mirror. "Probably too embarrassed."

If so, he'd been gentleman enough not to let it show. *When he hadn't been caressing her until she thought she'd melt.* She shook some of the water out of her hair and toweled it dry.

Unreliable and indiscreet, her big toe. Nick Atwell was as reliable as the Cavalry, and so discreet he'd acted completely unaffected by her provocative behavior. What had gotten into her? Gin? Fear? Loneliness? Gratitude?

No matter the excuse, she owed it to him to apologize, to walk out there and modestly ask his forgiveness. Then, to show no harm had been done, she'd chastely seal it with a kiss.

Connie groaned. *No* kisses. No matter how dewy-eyed she got, no matter how she admired him, the man was clearly as uninterested in playing lover as he was in playing hero. That he'd be wonderful in both roles made her nerve-ends zing. She started the shower again and stood under a stream of cool water.

"Get a grip, Hennessy. You are not going to fall in love with a man just because he's on your side. You are *not* marrying another Paul."

The thought of her ex-husband, another decent, risk-taking hero type, sent waves of regret washing over her. Paul Bianca was a Navy SEAL specifically trained in commando rescue missions. She' fallen in love with him precisely for that reason. Deep down, she'd wanted someone to help her save her father. He'd volunteered.

"You're not using Nick the same way. Damsels don't always go off with the knights who rescue them from dragons. Gratitude and sex are not the same thing."

He entered on the word "sex," his voice reverberating in the tiny bathroom. "Are you all right?"

"Don't mind me. Some people sing in the shower; I talk."

Those weren't the only things people did in showers.

Nick slung his jacket over his arm. The shower mist, added to the afternoon humidity, instantly drenched him from the inside out. His clothes stuck to him everywhere, including the stubborn bulge in his slacks.

His head hammered. His pulse throbbed in counterpoint. He wanted to make sure she was okay before he said good-bye. He wanted to be everything she thought he was. He wanted to touch her, but still had enough old-fashioned notions of honor to keep his hands to himself.

"Thank you for all your help, Nick. I don't know what I would have done—" Her body was a pink blur beyond the scratched plastic of the shower curtain.

"Be seeing you." He bit his tongue. "I'm going."

"Nick?"

"Yes?" With effort, he left off the "love."

"About this afternoon. Here, I mean." Connie was going to apologize if she choked on it. Hiding behind a curtain might help wizards from Oz, but she owed Nick better than that. She drew the curtain aside, modestly holding part of it across her body. "I'm sorry if I threw myself at you."

He raised a palm. "Already forgotten."

"Is it?" She laughed. "I should be insulted."

"You should be packed off the island before I do something we'll both regret," he mumbled, turning away.

"What was that?" She leaned toward him. The curtain suddenly adhered to her body, the plastic turning transparent on contact. Connie jumped back, peeling it off. "Sorry."

"For what?" He meant it, the anger, the frustration, all of it. The gravel in his voice should have warned them both.

What did she have to apologize for except being beautiful, being wounded, being determined and brave, and all the rest of it?

The curtain rings sang across the bar. Nick set one foot on the shower's threshold and wrapped an arm around her naked waist, crushing her slick body to his chest. His palm closed on her rib cage and his fingertips skimmed the underside of her breast. Her knees buckled.

"You don't have to apologize to me for anything. Ever. You're the bravest woman I've ever known and I—" Nick kissed her before he said any more. He kissed her lips, her mouth, kissed her body with his as he pressed her back against the wall, the water cleansing them both.

"You're fully dressed!"

He glanced down at his shoes, his slacks. Water plastered his shirt to his back. He memorized her body on the long journey back up. "So I am." He grinned and stole another kiss.

Her mouth opened. His tongue slipped inside like a thief, then a lover. The man knew exactly how far he wanted to go. Their breaths mingled, hot and damp on each other's faces. They broke contact and gazed into each other's eyes. Hers were as wide and green as the lagoon, as unfathomable as the ocean.

"Nick."

"Don't say no."

His lips followed the water's cascade down the side of her neck. His teeth toyed with the ridge of her collarbone. She gasped as he took her breast in his mouth. He was almost on his knees. Her fingers splayed on the wall at her back, her nails finding no purchase when her own knees began to give away. She moaned his name.

His hands came up the back of her thighs, memorizing the womanly fullness of her hips. Encountering her hands, he twined his fingers with hers, pressing her forward. His slacks absorbed the diamonds of water sprinkled on the glistening curls of her femininity. A thicker, warmer liquid stirred inside her. A shaft of heat thrust against her belly.

She shook her head, tendrils of wet hair clinging to her shoulders. "I want to give you this. Please. I think you need me as much as I need you."

"More." The word tore from him.

Unspoken promises passed between them, unspeakable doubts. Later she'd recall how he'd held her for a long moment, as if making up his mind. How he'd stepped back at last, looking down and away as if making sure of where the lip of the shower was. His eyes, an icy blue, focused on hers as he handed her out of the shower. For one heart-stopping moment she thought he'd lead her to the bedroom.

Instead, he waited until she reached the door. Then he reached into the stall, twirled the faucet to Cold, and aimed the showerhead until the icy needles soaked his front as thoroughly as they'd soaked his back.

"Better," he said lightly, slicking his hair back and knotting his saturated tie. He tossed his suit coat over his arm. "I'll call you tomorrow when I've figured out what our next move should be." With that, and a peck on the forehead, he strolled out of the room and out of her life.

Connie waited until she heard the door close, then sagged against the sink. She imagined his soggy shoes squeaking all the way down the hall. The man looked as if he'd just walked out of a monsoon.

"And you know what?" she said to no one in particular, "I bet the people at the embassy won't even lift an eyebrow." She laughed until the bathroom echoed with it. Her hero might be all wet, but he was still her hero.

She wiped a tear off her cheek. He was right, of course. She was in no emotional condition for what they'd almost done. One more kiss and she'd have been tumbling head over heels in love with the man.

Wasn't that what he'd been after? Why else would a man be so sweet, so tender, so suddenly bold? Why would a man leave?

Complicated relationships she didn't need. She'd come here determined to rescue her father. Instead she found her nights filled with dreams of Nick Atwell.

"I need you, Nick."

For minutes on end she allowed herself to think it might be for reasons other than his connections. She didn't know. Nitroglycerin wasn't so volatile as love and loss and loneliness mixed together. She indulged in one harmless daydream involving a thin roguish man, a bed, and a breeze stirring the curtains on a moonlit night. Then she toweled herself off and crawled into bed—alone.

Nick took the back way into the embassy, climbing the fire escape to his apartment in the rear corner of the building, too tired to face the looks he'd get if he didn't clean up first. This love business was exhausting. And pitifully one-sided.

"It'll stay that way," he vowed. Connie Hennessy had enough trouble without some lovesick Englishman trailing after her. Of course, there was no way he could tell her that. No emotional demands he could impose.

Just let one woman look at him the way she had today and he'd say his life had been well spent. It was almost a prayer, one doomed to go unanswered.

And yet, even if she couldn't love him back, couldn't even know, there were a hundred ways he could show his love for her. Saving her father would be one. Respectfully keeping his hands to himself was another.

"One is a damned sight harder than the other," he muttered. But which?

Nick stepped into his apartment and got out of his clinging clothes, ready for the lecture: He didn't deserve her; eventually she'd leave, with or without her father; he be a lying dog to lead her on.

Lecture over. Shower on.

Nick hung his head and let images of Connie wash over him with the spray. Futile really, all this talk.

He knew he'd touch her as long as he was near her, kiss her, treasure her. Under the circumstances, saving her father was the least he could do.

"What are those?" Connie asked.

"Koa-pora vines."

She shaded her eyes under the brim of an Indiana Jones hat Nick had handed her in exchange for the keys to the Jeep. He'd insisted on driving, crisscrossing the mountainous island on one muddy two-track road after another.

Connie had expected a grueling trip, but nothing had ever prepared her for Nick Atwell. Not for the first time, she ran a hand over the back of her neck and squeezed.

"Need a handkerchief?" He pulled a lavender one out of his jacket pocket.

Connie laughed. "Always the gentleman."

"Not always."

The banter evaporated. Time hadn't dissipated the effect of yesterday's encounter. It flared each time they inadvertently met each other's gaze, like a gust of hot air, sticking to the skin. Connie's neck prickled. She handed back the strip of silk.

Nick dragged it across his own forehead, dotted with moisture. Then he tapped it against his lips, inhaling her perfume. Realizing her eyes were on him, he hurriedly wadded it into his pocket. "So," he declared.

"So."

The engine idling in a hamlet of ten or so huts, Nick turned off the ignition and the jungle sounds resumed, bird calls muffled by dense trees and stifling air, the mix of children's voices as little ones ran between the houses, staring at the foreigners.

Long strips of fields tended by stooped figures swathed in rags dotted the valley floor. "Those are women?" Connie asked.

"The poorest of the poor. That's why this is prime rebel territory. Always has been."

Each woman carried a bamboo staff. "What are they doing with those sticks?"

"The vines need to be moved every few days or shoots grow into the earth and the planet uses its energy building roots instead of koa-pora fruit. At least, that's what I've been told."

Connie gave him a wink, hoping that teasing would ease some of their discomfort. "Thank you, Mr. Science."

"Not big on botany, eh?"

"I'm more interested in political science than natural," she replied, her mouth set in a firm line.

"How about unnatural?" He waggled his eyebrows.

She laughed. "How about a drink?"

He stretched an arm over the back seat to retrieve the canteen.

Lukewarm distilled water wasn't Connie's idea of refreshment. Watching Nick's shirt stretch taut across his chest made her mouth drier than ever. The night had been haunted with dreams of him.

"You first," he said.

She fitted her mouth around the opening and succeeded in dribbling precious water down her front. It soaked quickly into her blouse; the fabric clung. Fanning herself with one hand, she plucked it away.

"If you wanted another shower, we could have stopped at my place," Nick murmured.

Connie colored from her toes to her nose. Thankfully, anything above that was in deep shadow from the hat brim and the blazing sun. She dipped the brim so her eyes couldn't give her away. "Why have we stopped?"

"You looked tired. We've spent hours on this goose chase."

Hours avoiding talking about yesterday, Connie

thought. Hours losing a battle with restlessness and fatigue. Divided loyalties would do that to a woman. She had enough to worry about without wondering whether Nick would ever smile at her again.

Her father was a prisoner on this island. Did he know she was here? That she was looking for him and would never give up? Did he know there were times his daughter still needed his advice? Like right now?

"Let's go on," she said.

"In a minute." As if purposely ignoring her impatience, Nick leaned back. He cocked a heel on the dash, tapping the other on the far side of the brake. He poured himself a handful of water, running his palm across the back of his neck.

His hair grew long back there, a wave of black against his khaki collar, a tickling of strands across the top of his ear. Wetted down, it clung flat, mixing with the perspiration.

Connie shifted in her seat. Untapped energy irked her. Stopping at tin shacks and isolated huts while Nick talked with the natives, she'd had little to do except wonder and hope, indulging dreams of her father's release that she hadn't allowed herself to picture for years. She'd rush into his arms. Would he look the same? Have a beard? Had they given him new clothes? How thin would he be? Would he recognize her?

Her throat tightened.

"Connie?"

She looked toward the mountains looming over the valley, a deep, unreal green filled with shrieking birds, all of it blurring with her tears. Stooped women trailed in from the fields, their silhouettes wavering in the heat. "I want to run up to them and just ask them, 'Have you seen my father?' 'Do you know where he is?'"

Nick lifted her clenched fist to his lips and kissed

the back of her hand until her fingers relaxed. Her skin shivered despite the heat. Maybe because of it.

Nick dabbed another kiss on her palm. "We can't rush into this."

"No?"

"We have to make contact, take it slow."

He could have been talking about many things. He realized it, quickly breaking eye contact. "We'll ask around, let it be known we're looking, then see who comes to us."

"That could take forever."

"We've got time."

"Have we?"

Nick winced.

Connie looked away, trying to get the pleading out of her voice, the lump out of her throat. She already cared too much for Nick Atwell to use him. She couldn't impose on his kindness by mistaking it for love.

He couldn't know. *She* couldn't know. She'd lied to herself about loving Paul—maybe she was lying now.

The man was bored stiff on this island. He enjoyed the adventure she represented. Maybe. One wistful corner of her heart hoped otherwise. Maybe when all this was over, when her father was safe and she could have a normal life again, maybe she and Nick could meet without this tangle of obligations and reputations wearing each of them down.

A lot of maybes. A lot of dreams. Reality was finding her father. And hoping he recognized her.

Balancing her elbow on the door, she pretended to look at the village. Hastily, she wiped a tear off her cheek, blending it back into her hair with the sweat. "About yesterday."

"Did you sleep well?" Nick asked briskly. "Did the gin help?"

She sniffed, a wry smile on her lips. "As a matter of fact, it did. After you left."

His heel thudded to the hump on the floor, and he straightened in his seat. Nick resettled his hat on his head. He might as well face yesterday afternoon head on—and lie. "You were—"

"—overwrought."

He would have said *desirable*. "Yes."

"And overpowering."

He should have said *delectable*. "Perhaps."

"I'm sorry if I embarrassed you."

He could have said *I wanted you.* Instead, he said, "I overstepped the boundaries."

"I didn't see any boundaries," she replied softly.

Nick swung his leg out of the Jeep. "There she is. Excuse me a moment." He strode toward a bent old farming woman.

Unable to speak the language, Connie stayed behind plumbing sensations of relief and disappointment. Maybe he didn't care for any more involvement than the diplomatic challenge her situation offered. If he'd kissed her in the shower, if his eyes had darkened, his voice roughened, if his body had stiffened whenever she'd touched him, that was no more than a normal red-blooded man reacting.

She had higher priorities than falling in love. Bigger wishes than him returning her feelings. Last night's rebel activity had interrupted the electricity so often she'd awoken four times to a stilled overhead fan, her body glistening with perspiration. Each time she'd thought of Nick in the shower, how he'd held her slippery body to his.

Apparently, *he* had had no trouble sleeping through the distant barrage. Nick was used to danger. Nick was used to keeping his diplomatic distance.

They had no future, not in the real world. Connie pictured and planned on nothing beyond her father's first day of freedom. That had to be her only goal.

The vision of that day warmed her heart with a sweetness like pain. It blended with something new, the inevitable aftermath of leaving Nick behind.

Maybe that was the best reason of all not to trust her teetering emotions.

"One man at a time." She'd keep that thought firmly in mind.

Minutes later she found herself holding her hat in place after Nick had sprinted to the Jeep, gunned the engine, and tore away. The tires spewed mud all the way out of the valley.

"I never thought you would. You came out of that building like a trooper."

"But afterward," she repeated ruefully.

"You think I don't like a woman coming apart in my arms? It's the highest compliment a man can receive."

"You're being flippant."

"And you're being awfully earnest. We can dismiss this like two experienced adults. If that's what you wish."

But it wasn't, she thought morosely. "Nick, I've used people before. I may be using you, and I think it's only fair to warn you. Sometimes needing someone and using them become so intertwined that even I don't know which I'm doing."

Her confession didn't faze him. He plucked an umbrella out of his drink and folded it beside his plate. "Completely understandable in the circumstances."

"But not very nice."

"Neither is taking people hostage. I don't judge you, Connie. You're loyal to those you love. I can't say how much I admire that. I can't say how much your courage and your honesty mean to me."

"You're doing a pretty good job of it."

He toyed with her fingers. Desire flickered through her like the moonlight playing in the garden outside, promising.

He'd touched her too often for her to be surprised at her responsiveness. It was instantaneous, as swift as a startled flock of birds taking wing, soaring aloft on thin air, swooping on currents. Just the opposite of caged.

The image brought her back to earth, to the reason she was here. "You still haven't told me why we took off like that. I expected rebel Jeeps to come storming down the path at any minute, guns blazing."

"I half expected that myself."

Her blood chilled. Without realizing it, she laid her hand over Nick's. "Were we in danger?"

"We ran full tilt in the opposite direction. Best way to avoid it."

Connie's pulse quivered and a hollowness filled her lungs. "Did the old woman warn you?"

"Not in so many words."

"Did she say anything about my father?"

"No." Nick held back information by sheer force of habit; years of diplomacy had taught him to reveal no more than necessary. But he and Connie were in this together. She was doing everything she could for the man she loved; it just wasn't him.

He moved the candle aside and leaned toward her, lowering his voice. "The woman implied the rebels were nearby."

Connie clenched his hand. Warmth flowed up Nick's arm and glowed in his veins. He struggled with the idea that loving someone and deserving them were two separate things. If he had to pick up information this way to win her smile, her attentive eagerness, he'd gladly do it day in and day out.

"How close were we?" She meant to her father.

The candlelight reflected in her eyes, her pupils wide and dark in the sea of green surrounding them. Islands Nick swam toward. It was the first time she'd gazed at him so openly all day, the longing evident, unconcealed. Not for him at all. He smiled at the irony. "On an island this small your father is close no matter where we are. That doesn't mean he's free."

"Do you think he might have seen us?"

"Please don't get your hopes up."

She compressed her lips and nodded.

"No great expectations. Promise me."

She stared past him into the darkness and shrugged. "I've grasped at so many straws, what's one more?"

Nick gave her hand a quick and hard squeeze,

recalling the first time he'd seen her struggle with this same despair in Whitcraft's office. His heart had gone out to her then. Maybe it was time he faced the fact it wasn't ever coming back. "We work with reasonable assumptions, not rushing off at a mere rumor of his whereabouts."

"I'm not giving up."

"I know. That's one of the things I love about you." He missed her surprised glance. "However, you've more courage than caution. If I'm not careful, you'll tie a bandanna round your forehead and march up into those mountains like Rambo."

"But he could be up there."

"Or in a cellar. Or a fishing boat on the northern tip of the island. There's no telling, Connie. We keep looking, that's all for now."

Aware of prying eyes, Nick calculated his next move. No one could be allowed to see anything beyond the average seduction scene, the odd affectionate gesture. No one could guess at the words being said, or the emotion behind them.

"One more thing." He lifted her hand, kissing each of her fingertips in turn. Her nails were bare, short and rounded. Just long enough, he thought, to dig into a man's back. They dug into his palm when he finally spoke. "We know he's alive."

Connie let out a tiny gasp.

He put her little finger in his mouth and nipped the end. "No outbursts, Connie. No tears."

She swallowed, unable to comply with his last request. A riot of emotion cascaded through her. Her father was alive! She'd never doubted it, but hearing it confirmed made her heart swell. "Then someone knows where he is. Can I see him?"

"One step at a time, love. And try not to beam. People might think that beatific look is meant for me."

Her eyes crinkled with laughter and just as quickly

filled with tears. "Thank you," she whispered, her voice strangled and hoarse. "How do you know?"

"A sighting four weeks ago." He couldn't tell her where or she'd rush into those mountains for sure. They'd been close.

Moisture shimmered on her lashes. "You've done so much." She cupped his face, tracing a thumb across his lips in a gesture no one could misread. "I owe you a lot." She combed his hair back over his ear with her short nails.

He felt a streak of heat all the way down his spine. "Maybe tonight you'll get a good night's sleep at last."

"Will I?"

He should have heeded the warnings his body gave out, the tightness in his chest, the thrumming of his heart, the last remnants of idealism and honor that said he'd made a mess of his life so far and daren't ruin this. "You should."

"Maybe we both should."

He didn't answer.

She didn't let go. "There's something else we have to discuss. I've had the feeling you've been blaming yourself for yesterday when it was my fault."

"I won't hear it. A gentleman—"

"—is exactly what you are. Nick? I wouldn't have minded."

Heat flooded through him, the slow pound began in his blood. He would have blamed it on jungle drums, but that quaint tradition wasn't part of Lampuran culture. "I promised not to take advantage."

"You also said you'd help me."

"I'm doing what I can."

"You treat me like something fragile."

No, he thought, something priceless.

Deciphering the caution in his eyes, Connie was sorely tempted to bite *his* little finger. She played her teeth against his fingernail. Getting startled, stormy reactions from reserved Nick Atwell was too intriguing. She had a cause to which she was passionately committed. Finding a man just as passionate thrilled her. That he insisted on keeping it so firmly under wraps frustrated her in more ways than one.

"Nick, I apologize for yesterday. Honest I do."

The extra emphasis made him look up. Doubt clouded his face.

"The last thing I want to do is chase you away."

He laughed against his will. "Only a sharp pointed stick would accomplish that."

"I've been so alone in all this. To find someone who feels the way I do, who cares, it means everything to me. But what about you? I'm doing this for someone I love. You're risking so much to help a total stranger."

And sleep with his daughter, Nick thought.

"I'd call those pretty high motives," she said.

Nick grimaced. He'd given himself over to loving Connie Hennessy. As far as he was concerned, there was no higher cause.

"A woman could fall in love with a man like you," she said. "Women fall in love with heroes every day." Her gaze flitted to the table top, his shirt cuff. She curled her fingers around his wrist. His bumping pulse made her look up at last. "From what I've seen, you're not immune to causes and maybe you're not immune to me."

He swallowed, hard, as she held that galloping pulse. "It seems I can't stop giving myself away around you. It's a good thing we're on the same side."

She laughed, a breathy intimate sound that hushed over him like the night breeze. "We could be."

"If I'd rushed you yesterday, I'd have never forgiven myself."

"I might not have been ready. Yesterday."

His hand grew warm in hers, his grip tight. Too

many potent images filled the air, the remembered hiss of water against tile and mouth against mouth, the squeak of skin and the cling of his wet clothes. How a sharp intake of breath had pressed her breasts into his palms.

"I thought this would be a bad time for you," he said.

She laughed. "The last ten years have been a bad time."

"Has no one . . . ?" Too personal. None of his business. "I hate to think you've had to carry this alone."

"My mother worked very hard to give me a normal life. She insisted I date, do all the teenage things. But it was really a double life—normal only on the surface. Mom may have shielded me, but I learned a lot. Life is short; people sometimes lie. When you find someone you can count on, you hold on to them. If we had all the time in the world, I might wait before saying this . . ."

Unfortunately, they had no time to spare. George Cunningham strolled across the parquet floor, smiling blandly as usual.

When Connie discreetly released his hand, Nick used it to raise his drink. He needed this one. "Evening, George."

"Evening, Atwell. Miss Hennessy. I hear you've been touring our lovely island."

"We have," she said, a sunny smile beamed at him. The woman looked as if the clouds had parted at last.

Nick felt the heat.

"Good thing you've got Atwell as a guide. He knows all the hot spots."

"I'm sure he does." Connie slipped Nick a glance and wrestled with a grin.

Nick swallowed the last drop of gin and signaled for more.

"No run-ins with rebels?" George asked casually.

"A few army roadblocks," Connie replied politely. "Nick got us through."

Nick frowned at his fish, extracting a tiny bone. Connie wondered what she'd said wrong.

"Mm," George murmured. "You might want to look out for those. Army's as trigger-happy as the rebels lately."

"No fear," Nick answered. "Lovers on holiday attract very little attention."

George responded with a short grunt and bowed. "Enjoy your evening."

"You too, old man."

"Good-bye." Connie waited until Cunningham faded into the dim recesses of the restaurant. "Did I say something wrong? Did I?" Her eyes twinkled. "You said we were lovers. Wishful thinking?"

He wished that Mona Lisa smile of hers would fade. Why should it? The original hadn't faded in four hundred years—which was about as long as he'd love a woman with her spunk. "You told him we'd been in territory the army had sealed. He might draw conclusions from that."

"He's on our side."

"He's on the embassy's side. It isn't the same. You and I might have to treat with the rebels to reach your father."

"Do you think he suspects?"

"He wouldn't be George if he didn't. George suspects everyone."

They ate in silence. Nick felt vaguely guilty. And dissatisfied and edgy and more than a little put out. It was getting harder and harder to keep his distance, especially when Connie insisted on smiling at him like that.

"I'm no saint," he announced. "Put us together in a room and I couldn't be trusted not to— Well, I wouldn't want to test it."

Connie swallowed the rest of her drink. She wiped her lips with the crumpled napkin, imagining exactly what kind of tests a man like Nick put himself to. The tension in her body uncurled and another took its place. Sultry air flowed in and out of her lungs, her chest rising and falling, her breasts skimming the inside of the black chiffon she'd worn again tonight. Now she knew why.

He was trying so hard not to let it show, living the kind of double life she was so familiar with. She wondered why no one else noticed the lonely way he clung to ideals. Perhaps because no one else valued them the way he did. They noticed his isolation, and because of that, easily believed he took refuge in alcohol.

Absolutely no one but her saw through his act to the man inside. For a moment Connie wondered if that's what love was. The soft glow in her heart told her yes.

Nick ran a thumb across his bottom lip. "I know I'm second in line," he said gruffly. "You have your father to consider. I can live with that. For now."

Connie wished his hand remained on the table where she could reach it. A small voice warned her she might be making a fool of herself. But then, she did that every time she walked into an embassy and begged for help. All that experience came in handy when she reduced it to a simple equation: Nick, like her father, was a man worth fighting for.

A memory intruded; she voiced it. "People can be taken away from you so quickly. One minute I was a headstrong teenager arguing with my father about being grounded, and the next—"

Nick slanted a smile her way. "I can picture that."

"I threw a tennis racket after losing a match." She blushed becomingly. "Hormones, I think. I had a terrible crush on my tennis instructor, and when father grounded me for a week, I snuck out of the house and went to my lesson anyway."

Passionate even then, Nick decided. He relaxed against the booth, imagining Connie as a coltish, stubborn teenager with a mind of her own and more daring than prudence. "Did you get caught?"

The sudden bleakness in her eyes put his every nerve-ending on alert. "He did," she replied. "My father. Three men in masks seized him as he got out of the car. He yelled my name. Then he saw who they were and what they meant to do and yelled it again."

"You saw it all?"

"It was my fault."

His palm slapped the table. To hell with the staring. "What a handful of government thugs do is not your fault."

She lifted her chin. "It keeps coming back to that. If he hadn't been there— If I hadn't gone to that lesson—"

"They could have snatched him anywhere. You know how terrorists work. It was opportunism, plain and simple. Miserable bastards." He crumpled his napkin in his fist, barely aware of what he was doing, then stuffed it in his breast pocket. He pulled it out with a snort when he realized it wasn't his handkerchief.

Connie laughed as if the slapstick were for her benefit. "It's okay, Nick. I know it's illogical to think all this happened because of me. I shouldn't feel guilty, and I shouldn't carry it around with me." She shrugged, her hair glimmering across her shoulders in a warm red arc. "I can't help it."

Nick wrestled with the notion that he could make up for ten lost years of her life. It was as illogical as her guilt over her father's abduction. All the same, he longed to try, anything to erase that lonely look in her eye.

He said nothing. The words "I'll do what I can" caught in his throat like barbed wire.

Her voice was soft, almost hopeful. "Maybe after my father's free, when life returns to normal . . ."

"You'll go back to America."

"You don't have to be so blunt."

"The old woman hinted there might be a rebel movement afoot. I don't know when or where, but they're preparing a strike."

Connie's heart skipped a beat. "You didn't tell me."

"I only told the ambassador, and George."

"He didn't mention it."

"George wouldn't."

Her heart hammered and her skin grew clammy. "Oh, Nick. Every time the government changes hands, my father's in such danger. He could be freed, he could be—"

With a slight shake of his head, Nick gave her a silent warning. "It may have been disinformation. Things will get ten times more complicated when the shooting begins. I don't want us starting something we may never finish. One man who disappears is enough for any woman. You deserve someone who can promise you forever."

He wasn't that person. As if timed to underline the fact, the rebels chose that moment to detonate a bomb half a block away. Glass showered the inside of the restaurant, and the repercussion of the explosion was deafening.

"Stay down!"

Connie instinctively obeyed Nick's order, ducking under his arm as they crouched beside the embassy wall. They'd made it this far, but there was no guarantee they'd make it inside. The gate was locked and a hundred feet away.

The clatter of machine guns on the edge of town rattled like stones hitting a tin roof. The dull boom of anti-aircraft fire left round black clouds floating over town. It was like hiding from a fireworks exhibition, every rocket flashing white followed by an earsplitting explosion, but these firecrackers were lethal. Tracer bullets crisscrossed the Avenue de Charles de

Gaulle like lasers in a high-tech alarm system, cutting off the embassy from the capitol.

"It's a hundred feet to the gate," Nick shouted above the din.

"Let's run for it!"

Nick crouched beside her. "Not yet. I don't recognize that car." A rusty foreign sedan sat thirty yards away. "It could be wired with explosives. Besides, I don't relish standing outside waiting for somebody to let us in."

"What do we do?"

"Wait here."

A narrow concrete recess forced them to stand chest to chest as he shielded her with his body. For a crazy moment it reminded Connie of the shower. Then a high-pitched whistle screamed overhead and another bomb exploded at the end of the avenue.

In the flickering streetlight she could just make out Nick's face. He looked fierce, angry, his eyes an icy blue. His hands were over her ears. At first she thought he meant to protect her from the noise. Then his fingers tangled in her hair urging her closer. His lips pressed harshly against hers, slanting and savage.

"It'll be all right," he declared, his chest rising and falling sharply.

They stood together while the sky fell apart, fear and desire mixing in them like gunpowder, igniting in a burst of heat and flame.

"I love you," she shouted.

Another explosion obliterated his reply.

The headlights of a large black Mercedes blinded them as it swung around the corner. "Run like hell!" Nick shouted.

They used the car for cover, racing between it and the wall, sprinting through the gate as it swung open. They didn't stop until they reached the main building. Fifty feet behind them, the iron gate clanged shut. Oblivious of the aid he'd provided, the ambassador's driver headed for the underground garage.

One heavy knock from Nick's fist and the embassy door opened. The butler bowed, his bald head shining. "Good evening, Mr. Atwell. I take it your evening was eventful?"

In the sudden silence, Nick and Connie collapsed against each other, their ringing laughter interspersed with gasps of breath.

"Will you and the lady be needing anything this evening, sir?"

Weak with relief, Connie put her arms around Nick's waist and held on tight. "I don't know, do we?"

Nick shook his head, never taking his eyes off her. "No thank you, Jameson. We'll be fine."

"Very good, sir. I believe the embassy *is* the best place to be at the moment." The butler silently departed.

Connie plopped down on the marble staircase and laughed until tears came to her eyes. "There'll always be an England."

Nick joined her on the bottom step. "And what does that mean?"

"Are you all so unflappable?"

"Only in a crisis."

He kissed her sweetly, sifting a handful of hair away from her face. "Are you all right?"

She took inventory. She'd left her legs bare in the heat. She noticed it now because running had ripped the hem of her black dress, creating a daring slit and a suggestive breeze. "I'm fine. Couldn't run in these though." She swung her high-heeled sandals by the straps. "How are you?"

He didn't answer, sweeping a glance over her from head to toe. His hands followed the path his eyes had taken.

She examined his face. No cuts or wounds. A mouth tight with tension. A jaw clenched with anger. Fine lines of strain outlined his blue eyes. All of it caused by concern for her.

"I could use a drink," she said, meaning to ease his apprehension. Her voice came out husky instead.

His eyes darkened unmistakably and he stood. He straightened his shoulders and puffed his chest, getting that imperturbable look that said he'd be a gentleman no matter what.

Bushwa, Connie thought. Maybe she wanted to unravel him a bit. She let him help her to her feet and took one step.

"Why didn't you tell me?"

Connie jumped at his shout and followed his angry gaze to the vicinity of her feet. Blood was smeared across the bottom step. More slid beneath her feet. Her eyes widened. "I must have cut myself on the gravel."

"Or shattered glass. Or shrapnel."

"I didn't even feel it until now."

He swept her into his arms. "We've got to get you some first aid."

She regained her sense of humor midway up the second flight of stairs. Wriggling her hip against his abdomen, wrapping her arms around his neck, she drawled, "Mr. Atwell, has anyone ever told you you're a very romantic man?"

He grimaced and turned the corner for the third flight. "Are hernias romantic?"

Her outraged huff almost drowned out his groan as he took the last stair.

He staggered down a short hallway, twisted a door knob, and kicked open the door to his apartment. He stopped right there, a sober look on his face. "You know what it means if I carry you across the threshold?"

"That I get to see you in a truss?" She pinched his cheek.

He scowled and kicked the door shut behind them.

"Uh, Nick, you're not thinking of depositing me on some bed, are you?"

"Not some bed, *my* bed."

Six

The rumble of another shell made the building tremble. At least, Connie assumed that was the cause of her quaking head-to-toe. Nick's whole body vibrated as he very carefully held her away from him, kicked down the toilet seat, and deposited her on it. He'd quickly changed his mind about the bed and brought her in here.

Connie glanced around. "Now I know why the English call these water closets. Think this could be any smaller?"

"It has no windows to shatter."

"Good thinking."

In the glare and hum of a fluorescent light, Nick twisted the encrusted top off an old bottle of iodine. He fished out a couple of boxes of gauze from a cupboard.

Left to her own devices, Connie would've hitched one ankle on the other knee and peered at the bottom of her feet to assess the damage. She let Nick do the honors. He tossed a towel on the floor and knelt, gently manipulating her foot.

"It isn't a broken ankle."

"Putting off the inevitable. I hate the sight of

blood." Actually, blood didn't bother him the way the idea of *her* blood bothered him.

Suddenly, she touched his face. "You're going pale! Here, lie down." She stood, trying to reach a pile of towels on a shelf over his head for something to put her foot on. With him holding her other foot, she was as gawky as a one-legged pelican.

Nick stood, catching her solar plexus with his shoulder.

"Oomph!"

"Sorry, darling. No other way." He lifted her in a fireman's carry and, hands full of the iodine and bandages, carted her into the bedroom again.

"Where are we going?" she squeaked.

"Where I can have my way with you." He deposited Connie on his bed and scowled. "Bad idea, taking you where the light was."

"Be very, very careful how you say that."

"I simply meant, it's easier tending your wounds in here, but they look worse."

Connie lay back, but couldn't get comfortable while he ministered to her lower extremities. She had the linen apart in seconds, dragging down the coverlet and scrounging up a pillow for her head. She wriggled her dress to a nearly decent hemline halfway down her thighs and sighed. "I'm supposed to lie back and enjoy, I take it."

"Behave." Nick muttered as he dabbed at the cuts on her feet, employing a pair of tweezers. "You may have been right about the gravel. Your feet are filthy."

"Mom said that until she enrolled me in school, I never had clean feet. Wouldn't wear shoes."

"Stubborn even then, eh?"

"A hell-raiser."

"Can't be easy dealing with us diplomats."

"I've bitten my tongue so many times this last year I'm surprised I have one left."

Connie bit it again as Nick massaged her foot with

long gentle strokes of a warm washcloth. Sensations rippled up her body, which had no business bubbling to life while machine guns fired outside. The sporadic boom of shells faded beside the thump of her heartbeat. "Shouldn't you close the windows?"

"Don't you want to see the moon, darling?"

She gave him a drop-dead look, then lay back, sweeping her hair off the pillow and above her head, unbelievably relaxed. A beautiful moon hovered indifferently over the havoc. A puff of black smoke wafted across it. "There's a war going on, in case you hadn't noticed."

Nick clamped a strip of gauze between his lips, measuring and snipping as if this were an exact science. "Not a very efficient one."

"How do you mean?"

"The government's panicking. Why use anti-aircraft shells when the rebels only own two helicopters? As it is, the one's probably been cannibalized for spare parts for the other."

"Who do you think should win?"

"I don't much care as long as they treat people decently."

"Nice philosophy."

"Not much more I can tell you. Is that comfortable?"

Raising her leg, Connie glanced at his handiwork and wailed. "Even the Chinese don't bind women's feet anymore!" She twisted her foot left and right. "I could walk on hot coals and not feel a thing."

"Better safe than sorry. Speaking of which, this place is fortified concrete. We're fairly safe here."

"Fairly?"

"Unless a shell comes straight in that window, yes. Better to leave them open, rather than have them shatter."

"You think of everything."

"Just thinking of you."

That's what she was afraid of. It would be very

unfair to let him love her when she wasn't sure of her own feelings. She ought to dissuade him. Tell him right out they had no future. That idea alone made her want to revel in what little time they had. As their search narrowed in on her father, Nick's touch compelled her, comforted her, stoked fires that had no right being there but were.

"Now to get you in bed." Nick deposited the boxes and bandages in the bathroom and returned. "Under the covers, I mean."

Connie grinned. "Why is it I feel as safe with you as if we were on that moon?"

"Shock, I expect."

"Such a romantic." She laughed, a throaty pleased sound, and smoothed the coverlet. "Are you going to come over here and be safe with me?"

Nick flicked off the bathroom light. "We can duck in here if things get too hot and heavy."

"What things?"

"Connie."

"Planning another cold shower?"

"You think we'll need any with all this hullaba-loo?"

She shook her head, growing serious. "I saw the way you looked at me yesterday. And the way you tried not to let me catch you looking today. I think you've got me on some kind of pedestal."

"I've got you in my bed."

"Where I belong?" She rolled on her side and jauntily cupped her chin on her hand. "I know, I know. I'm being forward. You'll spank me next."

"I wouldn't touch that with— Never mind."

She grinned again.

He folded his arms and leaned against the bathroom door frame.

"Doorways are the perfect place to hide in an earthquake," she observed.

"Who's hiding?"

"Good question."

No deal. She wasn't goading him into lying next to her. If he went, there'd be no stopping this raging desire. It nagged at him, bullied him, flattered and sweet-talked him. He was a diplomat. He knew all the tricks for talking people in and out of things. He imagined talking her out of that dress.

He clenched his jaw until his teeth ached. How did a man fight a craving that strained at every inflexible, unyielding corner of his body? How did a man ignore love when it stared him right in the face?

When Connie's gaze faltered and began seeking corners, Nick's knees unlocked. She looked hurt, uncertain. She was so damn brave and so utterly convinced he was what she wanted that his heart went out to her. It was only a matter of time before his body followed.

"In the last ten years I've learned what really counts, Nick. Maintaining the status quo isn't it."

"I agree."

"Honesty is more important to you than playing by the rules. It's cost you a lot in your career. My father's freedom means everything to me. My mother tried to make sure his imprisonment didn't cost me my childhood."

"It had to."

"To some extent. I kept up appearances for her sake. Joined things at school. Dated."

"Married?"

She nodded. "For two years. Mom said if I ever found someone as good as my father, I should hold on to him."

Nick didn't reply.

"My ex-husband was that kind of man. He was plainspoken, down-to-earth, dedicated. But I was a cause to him."

Nick knew the feeling. He came over and sat beside her, running his hand down her waist, frankly resting it on her thigh. "Have I been doing that?"

She smiled sheepishly. "You tell me."

He squeezed her leg, skimmed it with his finger-tips, felt every goose bump rise and the flush of heat that followed like the sun coming up at dawn. "If you want me, Connie . . ."

"That's the problem. I want you, but I'm not sure."

He reassembled his heretofore unflappable reserve. "Then we shouldn't do anything you'd regret."

"I'd never regret you. What I'd regret would be using you. Hurting you."

"I believe I told you, I'm not as idealistic as I once was, nor as naive."

"No?"

He shook his head, and she reached up without thinking to comb a heavy black lock off his forehead. Her fingers strayed to just above his ear. He dipped his head. She gave her heart.

"Outside, you said something just as a bomb exploded. Would you say it again?"

Nick tasted iron on his tongue, a pure unadulterated taste that meant the time had come to lay their cards on the table. No hesitating, no lying. It wouldn't work anymore. This woman saw through him the way no one else did.

In an instant, neither of them saw anything at all. The main power station took a direct hit. Lampura City plummeted into darkness. Blackness fell between them like a curtain. Connie gasped and reached for him.

"I'm here." Nick's voice, close, harsh, startled her. His weight bowed the mattress. "I'm here, love."

She clutched his shoulder. For the first time, fear flickered through her. "Maybe we should hide in the bathroom." She waited for him to move. He stayed where he was.

"A touch of claustrophobia," he explained.

He snuggled closer. "I'd rather be here anyway. Wouldn't you?" He was doing his jolly voice, as if everything were one big adventure. It wasn't working.

Connie trembled when his hands conducted a thorough body check, caressing a bare strip of leg, her waist, skirting the underside of her breast to sweep up her arms, as if he had to reassure himself she was still beside him in the dark.

His nose bumped her cheek. His mouth traced her jaw. She felt him inhale when he nuzzled her hair. She lay back and he came with her, murmuring soothing words about how okay everything was going to be. Lord, how she loved him for that!

He caressed her hair again with his lips, every strand directly wired to the inner recesses of her body, the hidden places. Every surface was a secret shared, a landscape of intimate exploration. More soothing than arousing, he seemed intent on cherishing the outer limits of her body, testing the limits of his own self-control, and coming no closer than the edge of the bed.

Another shell hit. The foundation shook.

"How close was that?" she asked.

"End of the street." He sensed her tension. "It isn't like thunder, it doesn't get closer. The army's aim is extremely erratic."

"Meaning one could land on us any time."

The bedsprings jangled as he scooted down, touching hair that fell away from her temple, his breath humid as the sea breeze, warm as the tropical night. "I won't let that happen."

She shook her head just to feel his lips skim her ear, to hear her hair whisper and the breath feather out of his lungs. "Stay with me."

Her body felt hollow, her heart beat as if in a cavern. The unmistakable smell of gunpowder floated through the window, penetrating, sulfuric, insanely mixed with the lingering aroma of heavy tropical flowers whose petals had closed a little over an hour ago. All of it mixed with the scent of Nick, a musky scent she'd come to love.

The havoc outside intruded—shouting men, squealing armored cars. "Isn't there something we can do?"

Nick kept his tone deliberately light. "You and me? On a bed? You have to ask?"

She found his chin and pinched it. "I meant about that." A burst of gunfire obliged.

"Nothing at all, not until morning."

"Then what?"

"See who won."

"And who has my father. If the rebels take the capitol, they could bring him here."

Nick wrapped her in his arms. A long silence passed.

He stretched an arm above her head and found her hand, twining their fingers. His other arm rested on her waist, the chiffon of her dress silvery in the moonlight their eyes had adjusted to. Nick watched a tear form at the corner of her eye and slide silently away. Another followed it.

She stared at the ceiling as if she couldn't see him yet. The hurt in her eyes showed plain the longer he hesitated. "What did you say? Outside?"

"I said I loved you. It might have been the moment."

"Or the truth."

"I don't want to take advantage."

"Take it," she said fiercely. "Let me decide what I can and can't handle." She turned to look at him and another shameless tear slid away. "You think this is easy? Doing all this alone? Searching? Asking strangers for help?" Connie hadn't known the words until now.

"I needed someone, Nick. You were there. You have been since I arrived. You got mad at me for going into that cell. *I* bumbled into it, but you *knew* the risk. You came after me anyway. How can you blame me for loving you back?" She put her hand on his chest. "Say something."

He kissed her temple instead, the tears smearing,

his breath cool there, warm everywhere else. When his lips found hers, the words took care of themselves. "I love you."

"Say it again."

He'd say it a hundred times. The bombs might burst and the guns crackle, but the words rang true. "I love you."

She turned to him, rolling to her side so they'd be face to face. "When? How long?"

If he told her, she'd never believe him. Reasonable, sensible men didn't fall in love with women on first sight. Only on second, and third sight—and every time thereafter that she came into his mind or car or room. Unbeknownst to Connie, she'd been in this bed a hundred times since her arrival on Lampura.

"The smartest move I ever made in my life was falling in love with you," he said. "I've botched everything else by saying the wrong thing at the wrong time. I don't want to say it now."

"You can't go wrong with 'I love you.'"

He crushed her to him, wrapping her in an embrace that robbed her of all breath, all sense.

"Nick. Love me, make love to me."

He placed small, particular kisses along the ridge of her kiss-swollen lower lip. The harshness of their breathing melded in the dark, thrumming like the rockets outside. His mouth mated with hers, a penetrating yearning that aroused an answering response. Her tongue welcomed him, stroking the satiny underside of his until his body shuddered.

He took it no further.

Frustration warred inside Connie. She insinuated her body next to his, demanding with her kisses, her soft sounds and thwarted cries. She'd loved no man since her divorce. Even that hadn't been the kind of love that caught fire, stealing her breath away. She wasn't an expert in making love, but she'd learned to ask for what she wanted. "Nick, please."

"I don't know if I can protect you."

Connie smiled a woman's private smile. So thoughtful. "Are you talking about condoms?"

"The ones we have are as old as the iodine. They might break."

So might he if she didn't stop pressing into him like that. She insisted that few things in life really mattered. The love of a good woman was at the top of his list. Nothing and no one had made him want to change his life the way she had. But children, the most concrete of all futures a man and woman could share . . .

He imagined her belly swollen with a child, their child. He imagined a safe world, somewhere else on this troubled planet. The kind of places he couldn't get posted to if he got down on his knees and begged.

"What are you thinking?" she asked.

A man didn't tell a woman he wished he was more suited to his job at a time like this. Nick nipped the side of her neck, wasn't satisfied with that, and sloped a tender kiss across her collarbone to the swell of her breasts. Children would swell those, too. "I'm beginning to think you want me," he said.

Her laugh rumbled like the far-off sea. Then she sighed, the sound like a wave coming to rest on a beach, when his mouth found the rise of her breast. "How can you tell?" she teased.

"Maybe these?" His mouth formed a small O on her pebbled nipple as it strained against the fabric of her dress. She stiffened beneath him.

"Nick."

"Can we get this off?"

She sat up as he reached around her and found the zipper. He drew it to her waist following the disappearing indentation of her spine and decided that was far enough. He urged her back, sliding the dress down her arms as she reclined, baring pearly skin in the moonlight. "I was right. You are a goddess from the sea."

She touched his smile with her fingertips. He took

two of them inside then released them, glistening invaders.

The filmy cups of her slip weren't necessary as she reclined, nor the thin straps he guided in the direction the dress had gone.

"It isn't fair," she murmured.

"Life isn't fair," he agreed. "Your father's imprisonment, me stuck on this bloody island, you going."

"We've got each other."

"For now."

She slipped the knot all the way down his tie in one long motion. He gulped. She undid his collar button. "You've got too many clothes on. Better?"

He groaned. "You're teasing me."

"Maybe I am."

He took his revenge in a thoroughly ungentlemanly fashion, strafing her abdomen with kisses. That bunched-up cloth that used to be her dress would have to go.

"You first," she replied, as if reading his thoughts.

He stripped off his shirt. "Happy?"

"Mm-hmm." She ran her hands over him, rasping the black hair on his chest in twin circles around his painfully tight nipples. When she sat up, intent on tormenting him the way he had her, he moaned. He couldn't prevent her hair falling in an auburn cascade across his shoulder, or her teeth from inflicting a string of love bites along it.

He couldn't stop himself from loving her if he tried.

A lock of hair fell across his forehead as he bent to kiss her again. The glow of their lovemaking continued to warm her cheeks. He stayed in. She didn't seem to mind. She didn't know what he was thinking.

Unlike Connie, who asked questions straight out, Nick stopped and thought before he decided on three simple words. "What comes next?"

"You send me flowers, silly."

He laughed and, just for that, kissed her forehead. He slipped out of her, the first of what would be many partings, one of them final. He banished the thought.

Situating himself alongside her, he took the side nearest the window as if shielding her from the battle. The fighting had died down considerably. From the sound of it, the rebels had shifted to the far side of Lampura City.

The moon had moved, too. It cast a black diagonal across the bed, silvering Connie's body, casting Nick's in shadow. Divided already, he thought. "What happens when your father is free?"

"Thank you for saying, 'when,'" she murmured softly.

He clutched her hand. "He will be. Even if I have to—" A lofty, honorable, romantic, idiotic, and completely inescapable notion occurred to him, glowing in his mind like an ember. "And after?"

She hugged him. "With the two men I love the most, I'll be the happiest woman in the world."

Unbearably precious words. Nick fought down a surge of resentment, at himself, at the world. He'd not only fallen in love with a woman he didn't deserve, there was no way she or her father could stay in this political climate. No way he'd use her love to coerce her to do so. "You'll want to leave."

He felt her resistance the moment he said it, the stubbornness that had brought her this far.

"I could stay."

"I wouldn't want you to."

Connie felt cold, one goose bump chasing after another across her skin. She sat up to grab the coverlet, but Nick deflected her from pulling it farther than her knees.

He trailed his fingers up her legs, pausing briefly on the pale skin of her thighs. He pressed lightly and she parted them. "I won't let you stay," he said, "not as some kind of payment for freeing your father."

"You think that's why I did this? Why we—"

He stroked her honeyed skin, so smooth, sweet, and sensitive. His fingers found her core and she gasped. "I can give you this," he said raggedly, his touch more explicit by the moment. His body pressed hers back. His fingers found their entrance and took their time.

"You said it yourself, Connie. When you love someone, show it. You never know when people will be taken away from you. With your mother gone, you can't send your father back to America alone. You'll have to go with him."

Her mind fought his words, but her body surrendered. "No," she said over and over. No to fate, no to politics, to every intractable, incomprehensible war. No to good-byes that should never be said, not at moments such as this.

She ignited at his touch. Minutes ago, when they'd first made love, her body had found its release in long undulating waves that shook her like the rolling surf. Her climax had been nothing compared to the tremors that had shaken him, his plunging thrusts, his powerful surrender. She'd experienced something sweeter, the joy of receiving him, of wrapping her silly bandaged feet around his hips and welcoming him deep inside where a woman gave a man everything she had to give.

This time was different. This was for her. There was no hiding, no joining. He drove her, his thumb scraping across her sensitive nub. "No," she pleaded, arching against him. *No, never let it end.*

He draped a thigh over hers, resting his chest on her breast, pinning her to the bed when she would have moved, would have begged to have him in her.

"Not this time," he breathed. His mouth swallowed her cries. She couldn't resist it, couldn't change the way things were, not the world, not the truth, not the rushing fury of sensations rocketing through her, trailing fire. Not the panting, falling sensation as the trembling ceased.

He spoke before she could argue, before coherent thought could make itself felt, and with it doubts and dreams and should-have-beens. "I can't give you a future, Connie. I love you. Know that. Whatever happens, I want you always to know that. Promise me."

"I do."

"We can't live together. No. I've thought it through and there's no way. After you've gone, no matter how far apart we are, no matter what separates us, remember I loved you. Will you do that?"

She couldn't understand the tears flooding her eyes. It was just love talk. Bittersweet words in the dark. She wanted to say the same things and, at the same time, didn't even want to think them. "I'll always love you."

He kissed her on the nose. "So you say now."

She laughed weakly.

"Marry anyone you like. Marry your ex-husband for all I care. But don't throw your life away on me. This isn't meant to be."

"Nick."

"There are better men. I want you to find one and be happy."

"There are telephones, you know. And faxes. And airplanes."

"And there are times to say good-bye."

She sat up, struggling out of his arms and into the suddenly chilly night air. "We can work this out."

"We have to find your father first."

"But after—"

He shrugged, pulling a pillow across the bed. Connie knew she should have been angry. For a moment she had been. She couldn't understand where this frightened feeling had come from, the sick woozy kind that seeped through her veins. She had enough worries without getting paranoid just because he wouldn't meet her gaze. "Nick?"

He commandeered both pillows and laid his head on his linked hands, indicating his chest with his chin. That would be *her* pillow. "I'll make a deal with you. After your father is free, we'll talk about the future."

He said it as if the answer would be obvious then. As if he had no fear he'd be proved right, and she'd calmly pick up and leave him.

Somehow his complete confidence on that point made Connie feel infinitely better. The man obviously had no idea what he was up against. She'd spent the last few years of her life negotiating. She'd learned from experts. She'd get her father. Then she'd get her man.

Seven

He insisted on carrying her to the bathroom when she tried to get out of bed.

"Are you going to carry me everywhere?"

"Maybe I'll keep you flat on your back until your feet heal."

"By then *you'll* need bandaging."

The image of a certain portion of his anatomy as thickly swathed in gauze as her feet, made them both laugh.

When he carried her back to the bed, Connie glimpsed her shoes beside it. "You going to carry me to my hotel, too? I'll never get those sandals on with these." She paddled her big white feet.

"I never realized you were running with them off or I would have carried you to the embassy."

"I'm glad you didn't. I'd hate to be one of those oh-I-twisted-my-ankle heroines from the movies."

"Never." She was too real for that, too committed and unrelenting. Unfortunately for him, so were the rebels they were up against.

He reached over the side of the bed and picked up one of her sandals, sniffing lightly.

She wrinkled her nose.

"Sexy," he insisted.

"A shoe fetishist! Now he tells me."

"There aren't many things sexier than two tiny strips of leather passing themselves off as support. I have a theory that a woman's shoes are clues to her choice in lingerie." He dangled the shoe over the bed. "Am I right?"

Connie wanted dearly to debate him on that point, but after their tedious sojourn in the mountains this afternoon, she'd leapt at the chance to go to her hotel room before dinner and change into slinky shoes *and* slinky lingerie. She'd told herself she was outwitting the heat, but cotton would have been more practical. Cotton, however, wouldn't sit on the corner of the end table in a tiny puff of lacy shadows. "You may have a point," she conceded.

"Generous in defeat too."

"On the rare occasions when I'm wrong."

"The rare occasions when you admit it."

"Was I wrong about us?" She slid her body along his; like the light spilling into the room, she was ghostly, ethereal, yet as real as the salty ocean scent wafting over them.

Outside, tracer bullets whizzed through the streets. A flare lit the night sky, a red arc slicing the moon in two. Neither of them noticed.

The other shoe dropped.

Later, they argued. Connie's stomach knotted but she refused to be swayed. Determination in the face of love was her strongest suit. "I'll stay."

"You may love me, but you can't love this place, Connie. Not after what it's meant to your family."

"I can make up my own mind."

He silenced her with a touch, dipping his finger in the bend of her leg, making her muscles tremble. "I won't make you a hostage of love."

"How about a slave of passion?"

"Ah, now there's an idea."

She brought his hand to her waist, no higher, no lower. "And if we don't find my father? What do you and I do?"

"Shh." He returned to kissing her hair. "We'll find him. I already have an idea how to free him."

"Tell me."

"We'll discuss it during all that time we have to waste in public. When we can't do this."

He did something sure to get them arrested outside the privacy of his room. Connie felt her fears ebb. At the same time, she felt as close to a man as she'd ever felt, as she'd ever feel again. "I never had a chance to tell him I was sorry, Nick. To tell him I loved him."

"I'm sure he knows."

"Does he?"

"Yes."

Later still, dawn tinged the sky a decadent shade of indigo, a soothing shade of blue, a sensual shade of rose.

"Say you love me," she whispered, their bodies joined.

Words, Nick thought. His life revolved around decoding them, glossing over them, making them say as little as possible. But love could be shown in more ways than one. He loved her more than he could say, beyond anything he'd imagined himself capable of. He'd show her how much.

"Even if it's the last thing I do," he murmured.

Around six A.M. Nick snuck out of bed, gently maneuvering Connie's head onto the body-warm pillows. He covered her with the sheet and dressed quietly.

The embassy's polished wood floors shone in the early morning light. Outside, birds sang. The smell of Lampura in the morning was like a drug, enveloping all the senses in a heady tropical haze plus the promise of heat. Reminiscent, thought Nick, of a woman in a warm bed.

Entering the radio room, he cleared off traces of last night's numerous cables alerting the world and their sister embassies to yet another rebellion on Lampura. He disliked this cramped, airless room, jammed with an ancient radio set, a computer, and coding machines. Nick set down his latest cipher and worked out the wording of his request.

He loved coding almost as much as decoding, making sense of camouflaged, purposely recondite phrases, watching the meaning unravel once he figured the game out. He'd even invented a few codes of his own, tricky, playful, quirky. This part of his life he shared with very few people, diplomats like him in other rooms like this in other corners of the world, people he'd never met and, if his plan succeeded, probably never would.

The heart of the message took up three words: "Locate Paul Bianca." Nick looked at the letters as he printed them out. Connie had told him all about her ex-husband last night.

"He was a SEAL," she said, snuggling beside Nick in bed.

"He liked swimming?"

She poked him in the ribs. "No, he was a SEAL. It stands for sea, air, and land capability. They're Navy-trained commandos. Go anywhere, do anything. They like to think they're tougher than the Marines."

"Ah."

"A lot of what they do is covert. Very hush-hush."

"Hush-hush," Nick murmured, liking the way the words sounded against her hair. "And how did you meet? Underwater somewhere?"

"In Washington. My mother and I appealed for a rescue attempt before a private Senate subcommit-

tee. Maybe *Rambo* had just come out, I don't know.
We'd tried everything."

"And him?"

"Paul. Paul Bianca. Very handsome, very honorable. About eight years older than me and twenty
years ahead in life experience. I was twenty-one at
the time."

Twenty-six now, Nick thought, his mind drifting,
imagining her as a younger woman, in Washington,
among all those monuments.

"Are you awake?"

"Awake and alive. Go on."

"He escorted me around town, showed me the
monuments."

Nick grinned to himself.

"I thought I was in love."

"Weren't you?"

"I fell in love with him the day he told me he
thought he could rescue my father. It wasn't until
after we'd been married that I realized what I'd done.
He was a good man, Nick."

"Any man with the sense to love you would have to
be."

"I felt terrible about how I'd misled him. And
myself. He made it easy on me when he saw it
wouldn't work, and we divorced. I used him."

"Use *me*." The harsh intensity of Nick's words
surprised them both. "Use me, Connie. I don't fool
myself that we can have more than this. All I want is
to make you happy. And for once in my life to be of
some earthly good to somebody. To you and your
father. In a way, I knew it the minute I walked into
Whitcraft's office that first day. If I can do good—"

He stopped, his mouth a tight line, his eyes seeking the ceiling as he considered the idealistic folderol
he'd just spouted.

Connie chuckled softly. "If those dodoes in the
Foreign Office had any idea about this swashbuck-
ling Robin Hood side of you, they'd be amazed."

Nick had to laugh, at himself, at the mess this was fast becoming. If he could hold on to one thing, his love for Connie, he could untangle all the rest. There had to be a way.

There was. It had come to him shortly after midnight. He'd been thinking he'd save her father if he had to walk up into the mountains and do it himself. The notion wasn't so farfetched. A man could go over to the rebels at any time. Coming back in one piece was the trick.

Back in the radio room, Nick finished his message and sent it. Wanting his dispatch received and immediately understood, he sent it in a popular code nicknamed Oliver Twist for its contorted but simple structure. Harry would have it figured out in ten minutes. Nick waited twenty. If he'd been a smoking man, he would have run through half a pack.

Locating Paul Bianca shouldn't be that difficult. Connie had remained friends with her ex-husband; she claimed he was still a member of that elite force. Both those pieces of information had locked into Nick's plan like tumblers on a safe, until he knew exactly what he had to do.

For a few minutes a jab of jealousy pricked at him. If Paul Bianca had been so wonderful, why had he let Connie go?

"Isn't that what you're planning to do too?" Nick's voice landed dully in the paneled room.

He had a plan that required an honorable, daring hero to carry it out. The man he'd always wanted to be. The kind who'd once married the woman he loved—but couldn't hold on to her. Neither could he.

Nick glanced up when an electronic beep sounded: Message Received. He tapped his pencil against the table a couple times and went back to bed. Back to Connie.

Connie liked to sleep with something on, a sheet, a comforter. Gradually it dawned on her that the heaviness of the morning air was the only thing lying on her skin.

Nick came back in and began to undress. "No more," he muttered when she ran her fingertips down his back. A fake scowl furrowed his forehead.

"I wanted to welcome you back to bed. Any more news?"

"Only what we've been handing out. I got called downstairs to fashion some diplomatic response to the crisis, then we sent all the journalists back to their hotel."

Duty called and he answered. Didn't they see? Connie wondered. Didn't the people in the embassy know that every time they turned to him, he responded? He handled their trickiest problems, and they gave him no credit at all.

"Nothing more than the usual," he added.

He gave himself no credit either. "As usual as this?" she asked. She ran a hand down his spine as he sat to untie his shoes. "Does anyone know I'm in your bed, Mr. Diplomat?"

She teased him unmercifully, sweetly learning every inch of him, playing over his skin with deceptively delicate touches, thinking mistakenly that she might seduce him with slow flames. But gentleness was a form of self-control. When that gave way, the desire behind it astonished and delighted them both.

For a man who wrapped his words in long crafted sentences, their conversation quickly dwindled to a few telegraphic commands. "Here." "Oh." "Please." "Again." Then words fell away.

She'd lost track of who was beholden to whom. Who led in kisses? Were they neck and neck on endearments? How many times had they made love? She probably wouldn't be able to walk, but after the way Nick had bandaged her feet, she'd toddle anyway.

She swallowed a laugh and felt tears close behind it. This couldn't end. When they saved her father—

Like dawn, the picture formed slowly in her mind.
Her father would meet Nick right away, probably on
the day he was freed. Nick would stand beside her
when the rebels released him. She'd hug her father
tight and tell him how much she loved him and how
long she'd waited for this day. Then she'd introduce
him to Nick.

He'd approve.

And Connie would find a way, through all the
rebels and diplomats and red tape in the world, to
stay with the man she loved. Because she did love
him. It wasn't a question of using anymore, it was a
question of keeping.

Nick had sent over to the hotel for her running
shoes. The laces removed to accommodate her bandages, Connie listened to the soles flop as she and
Nick picked their way through the wreckage of
Lampura City. Most of the buildings were newly
pockmarked by bullets, but only one or two had been
shelled. Their gaping facades looked incongruous on
such a brilliant sunny day. When they rounded the
corner to the Imperial Hotel, Connie exhaled a
pent-up breath to see it still standing.

Nick gave her elbow a squeeze. "I told you it was
fine."

"Will I be safe here?" she asked minutes later as
they entered her room.

"Wrong question." Nick closed the door, then the
curtains. "Will *we* be safe here?"

They were in each other's arms. But the mood had
changed. Seeing the destruction in the city made
Connie frantic to get back to the countryside, to find
out if the rebels were any nearer, if her father was
with them, what their plans were.

Nick sensed her unease. "Why don't you wash up
and change? I'll meet you back here in an hour and
we'll see where we go from here."

Her heartfelt "Thank you" pierced him like a rose's thorn. He treasured every pang, memorized every smile. "It'll be all right," he said, knowing his promise was empty. Once more he vowed that if he had any control over anything at all, he'd see to it her father was freed. "Trust me?"

She nodded up at him, no hesitation, no forced cheer. Her simple response made him swell with pride. As long as Connie loved him, there was no risk he wouldn't take. But she couldn't be part of it.

"You stay here," he said. "Don't come to the embassy looking for me. I'll be back in an hour at the most. If I'm not, ring George. Don't go out yourself."

"Are things that chaotic?"

"We won't know for a few days. What I do know is that you'd be a prize hostage. You go nowhere without me from now on. Understood?"

"Aye aye." She stood on her tiptoes and kissed him. "Come back to me."

"I will."

Four days passed in fruitless searching and warm, entangled nights. Monday afternoon provided one frustrating encounter after another. Connie and Nick drove slowly up and down the rubble-strewn streets, talking little, silenced by the destruction and anarchy following the repeated rebel raids. Passing through army barricades in any part of the city became a lesson in diplomacy and tact.

"They want to know if we're rebels." Nick sighed, returning from another outpost. "No one else would desire to leave the city, they say."

"*I* desire it. Tell them who I am. This is a mission of mercy. It's beyond their politics."

Nick took her hand and lifted it to his lips, distracting her with his gentle kiss. "Connie, they don't care. If he's with the rebels, he's a rebel."

"But he's not!"

Nick held her in his arms. The long nights were showing on them both, the intermittent shelling, the elation of their coming together. The arguments about what they'd do when they found her father, so abstract in the dark, came back in force in the light of day, ugly and real as the scrawny chicken pecking through a garden a few feet away. Lampura City was in tatters, and Connie's father was just another victim.

"What do we do now?"

Frustration edged through Nick like a rusty blade. "We go on."

"But how? We can't even get out of town."

"I know a bar."

"Nick."

He laughed at her chiding tone. "Bars are the best places to asked questions. Drink loosens tongues, especially koa-pora. Come on."

They drove back the way they'd come.

"What about that old woman in the hills," Connie asked as they veered around the burned-out hulk of a parked car into a section of the city she'd never seen, lined with bleak houses of corrugated tin that blazed in this heat. "She gave you good information a few days ago."

"As a matter of fact, it's her son we're going to see."

"Will he help us?"

Nick placed his hand over hers as her fingers curled on his biceps. "He might."

"Who is she?"

"One of the richest peasants on the island."

"You're kidding!"

"Thanks to rebel activity, a lot of women become widows at an early age. The old woman buys their land so they can start new lives in the city. Most hate it. When they return she puts them to work tilling their own land."

"Very enterprising."

"She owns most of the valley now."

"Whose side is she on?"

"I wouldn't want to say."

"You can trust me, Nick."

"Can I?" He pulled to a halt in a dusty intersection bisecting a cluster of abandoned houses. He wanted to talk to her, reassure her, watch the line between her brows fade. They'd been so wrapped up in their search, he'd neglected to tell her he loved her during all of the past two hours.

His idea didn't seem such a good one anymore. If he made a deal with the rebels, she'd leave the island with her father. He couldn't risk her coming back for *him*. Maybe he should lay the groundwork for their separation now, no matter how much it hurt.

He killed the engine. The acrid smell of smoldering fires hovered over the deserted streets. "I won't hold you to anything we've said in the dark. What people say, especially in dangerous situations . . ."

She turned abruptly away, staring out the side of the Jeep. Nick gripped her wrists. He had to make her listen, but all his tact wouldn't let him lie to her.

"I meant what I said then, but perhaps not in the way I said it." Good Lord, he sounded like Whitcraft tripping over his own tongue. "I do love you." There was no getting around that. "As for anything long-term, I don't envision us in a rose-covered cottage and I don't think you do either. I don't see myself getting off this island anytime soon—unless they completely remove me from the Foreign Office."

Which they'd no doubt do if they had any idea what he had planned, Nick thought.

Connie said nothing, implacably staring over her shoulder. Nick hated to imagine the tears streaking her face. At the moment, he hated the sound of his own voice, but he couldn't stop talking.

"You'd hate it here. I'd feel responsible. There'd be recriminations, regrets. Your father can't go back to America alone—"

"Nick?"

"Yes?"

"I think you'd better stop talking."

She turned, settling back in her seat, her chest sinking as she exhaled slowly. For a moment all Nick saw were her eyes, empty and green. Then he saw the army patrol emerge man by man from the empty houses. Rifles at the ready, they surrounded the Jeep.

Eight

It was like watching a cobra uncoil, Connie thought, transfixed by six men clothed in combinations of green and khaki shirts, American jeans, and running shoes with bright orange basketballs on the side. At a sign from one of them, three more men stepped out of a house directly to her right. In their center, a smallish balding man studied Nick and Connie with black glittering eyes.

He wore a neatly pressed white shirt hanging out over his loose slacks. He could have blended in anywhere in Lampura City. Only the deferential way everyone here treated him differentiated him from others in the group. That and the fact he was the only one not carrying a gun.

"Stay here." Nick inched his way out of the Jeep.

Triggers cocked. He froze.

Connie's heart thudded; breathing meant dragging in tiny gasps of air. "Don't go," she said.

Nick put one foot on the road then slowly swung the other through the cut-out door of the Jeep. "Let me do the talking."

A soldier yelled. Nick kept moving.

"What did he say?" Connie demanded.

"Stay here."

"Nick!"

"Don't worry, don't look afraid, and don't say anything. Okay, love?"

Not okay. Connie's blouse was drenched in sweat, her hands trembled. None of that distracted her from the most important thing: Nick wasn't beside her anymore. She'd seen these expressionless faces before. These men had a cause and nothing else, a cause that bleached the world of humanity in the name of politics. "Nick!"

He flashed a nonchalant smile at the crowd closing in on him, betraying not a speck of nerves. "I assume none of you chaps speak English or your commands would have been delivered in it." He spoke to her without turning his head. "Hence, we can speak freely, darling, as long as we keep our voices even."

Connie wanted her feet on solid ground. She wanted her hand in Nick's no matter what. "You told me to go nowhere without you. I'm sticking with you, Atwell. Got that?" She fixed a wooden smile on the three men in charge and started to get out of the Jeep.

Sliding around to the passenger side, Nick adeptly blocked her way before she could hop out. Orders given in the staccato Lumpuran dialect were suavely deflected by Nick's easy drawl. He stalled them, charmed them, changed the subject, all the while keeping up an ongoing translation/commentary so Connie understood every twist in the conversation.

"Do we carry passes, he asks. No, I replied. Are we man and wife? Not at present. What right do we have to be here? We're looking for a bar, I explained."

The man spit out a Lampuran expletive.

"Very well," Nick said, "I'll say we're surveying the damage. Considering how tense everyone is, I'm assuming last night's incursion must not have gone the government's way."

"Do you think the rebels are nearby?" Connie

asked urgently. "Have they moved my father closer to the city?"

"And who is your father?" the bald man asked.

Connie's heart caught in her throat.

Nick dropped the relaxed facade and drew himself to his full height, arms crossed over his lean frame. "You speak English."

"I'm sorry, Nick," Connie moaned under her breath.

"No harm yet, darling."

The bald man's voice was clipped, reedy and unpleasant. It made Connie's skin crawl. "You show some concern for the rebels' cause. What was your opinion of the battle?"

"We're not qualified to say," Nick answered smoothly.

"You are American." The bald man looked directly at Connie.

Her hand squeezed Nick's arm.

"Careful, dear," Nick murmured, reaching into his inside suit pocket. Guns came up. He pulled back his lapel and extracted a business-card holder. "I'm with the British Embassy, a subject of Her Majesty, the Queen." He handed over the entire gold case.

"And the lady?"

"Is with me."

"Perhaps she'll answer differently when questioned alone."

Connie kept her death grip on Nick's arm. She'd never seen this side of him. His easy smile had slipped at the corners, an icy self-possessed man took his place, focused, calculating. "I'm sorry, that would be rather inconvenient."

"Your convenience is not our concern." The bald man opened Nick's case and let all the cards flutter into the mud. He squelched one with his cowboy boot. Water seeped into the square-toed impression.

He smiled at Connie, his teeth browned by the local tea. "Do you approve of the government, Miss—?"

Connie knew from Nick's warnings her name alone

would make her a prime prisoner. What could Nick do to prevent them taking her? What would they do to him if he tried?

"Don't answer," he said sharply. "You're a foreign national. We've strayed into the wrong side of town looking for a place to have a quiet drink. There's no more to tell."

Connie had every intention of following Nick's lead until a sickening thud made her whirl. One soldier struck Nick on the back with his rifle butt, another proceeded to drag him away. He staggered, one wrist bent behind his back.

Connie screamed his name.

Nick's voice grated through clenched teeth. "Don't make any comments about the government!"

Connie didn't care. She wanted Nick. Ten feet separated them. Eight guns. To fight was impossible. Not to fight unthinkable. As he wrestled with his captors, an image came back to her as sharp and clear as a bayonet's blade in the sun. She remembered the way her father had backpedaled as they'd led him off, his shoes black and scuffed. The image infuriated her. Feelings of helplessness threatened to engulf her. She'd been helpless then. She wouldn't be helpless again.

"Your name please?" the commander requested.

Connie kept Nick in the corner of her eye. "I won't say anything if you take him away. Stop hurting him!"

The bald man muttered a word and flicked a cigarette into the mud beside Nick's business cards. The order was relayed; the men stopped. Nick started to say something, to shout another warning. A rifle butt connected with his abdomen. He dropped to his knees.

Connie's blood turned icy and thin. She turned to the bald man, her gaze frigid. Somehow she convinced herself they'd get out of this nightmare if only she could keep her voice calm. "What do you want to know?" she asked.

"Do you think the government was right to shell their own city to defeat the rebels?" the man asked.

"Are they defeated?"

"Your opinion, please."

She couldn't look at Nick. The sound of his labored breaths made her quake with fury. She folded her arms and stared at the ground, distracted again by those cowboy boots. She shook her head and tried desperately to concentrate. Her father's shoes, Nick's shoes, what did shoes matter? Because they did, she realized all at once.

Her head snapped up. "I believe the shelling proved the government cares nothing for the people. The rebels are the only ones working for the people of Lampura."

"Connie!"

Nick's anguished shout almost undid her. Her father had called her name like that. She straightened her shoulders and let the bald man's birdlike eyes peer into hers. "The rebels are very brave. My father is with them."

"Your father is William Hennessy."

"He is."

"Does he wish to be with the rebels?"

"I don't wish him to be. I want him freed."

"Connie, for God's sake, shut up! She doesn't mean it." Nick ceased his struggling when the muzzle of a gun tilted his head back. There was no thud this time, no hammer cocking, just an endless moment in the midday sun.

Connie's mouth went dry. "No one is who they seem, remember, Nick? These *are* the rebels."

The bald man extracted another cigarette, a cellophane pack crackling in his hand. "Your woman friend is a very astute observer. Release him."

Three thugs dragged Nick to his feet and shoved him at Connie. He stumbled to a halt in front of her.

Instantly recovering his poise, he straightened and slicked back his hair, hiding a wince at what that did to his bruised abdomen. "Are they indeed?"

Connie bit back a laugh too close to hysteria. "People are so poor here that young men cherish their army boots, *if* they're in the army."

"Not us," the bald man replied.

"You're pretending to be the army to see who's on your side," Nick said.

"Correct again."

Nick whistled low, taking Connie's hand. "Good thinking, darling."

"I had to do something." Now that the immediate danger seemed to have passed, tears threatened to choke her. She squeezed his hand as tight as possible. "Don't worry, they can't take me hostage."

"That you cannot know," the bald man challenged.

"We passed a real army patrol in the next square over. If they heard shots, they'd know you're still roaming the city."

The bald man laughed. "Is it you who threaten us now?"

"I want my father."

No one moved. The bald man spoke Lampuran to his aide, aware of Nick's careful listening. "Do you approve of her plan, Englishman?"

"No."

Connie whirled. "Nick!"

"I'll explain later. I'd rather we spoke privately, sir."

The bald man crooked a smile at Nick's request. "You may call me Colonel. We can speak in here."

Nick didn't spare a glance at the dark interior of the cramped house the Colonel had emerged from. "Sorry, I prefer the outdoors. Lampuran will be private enough."

The men spoke for ten minutes as Nick proceeded to spell out his conditions. Connie gathered as much from the way he numbered them on his fingers. She heard her father's name and made out pidgin references to the British Embassy.

Nick ceased speaking.

The bald man nodded. "We will consider your offer."

Nick handed Connie into the Jeep. The circle of men melted into the shadows and the shelled houses. The car started, a whiff of exhaust drifting past them.

When they found a road they both recognized as leading back to the Imperial Hotel, Connie let the air flood out of her lungs. Tension eased in muscles weakened by the effort of holding it all in.

"That was easier than I thought," Nick muttered to himself.

"Will they let me see him?" she asked.

She studied Nick's profile, the hard set of his jaw, the sudden cant of his smile when he stopped the Jeep in front of the hotel and lifted her chin with his fingers. "Maybe in a few days. We're getting closer. Although that was a little close even for me."

She threw her arms around his neck and gave way, a sob shuddering through her. "Oh, Nick. But what did they say? What were you saying back there? What was that all about?"

Me loving you, he thought.

"Were you making a deal with them?"

"As a matter of fact, I was."

Throwing open the windows in a vain attempt to get some fresh breezes to chase the stale air from her hotel room, Connie couldn't stop her mind from spinning or the words from tumbling out. "We could have gone with them."

"They weren't going back to the mountains, not yet."

"Is that where he is?"

Nick tried to calm his own racing heart, but the ache wouldn't go away. Although he loved her beyond sense, he thought he'd long since accommodated himself to the fact she cared about her father first. But apparently not, for unreasonable flashes of envy goaded him. "The rebels must believe they've gotten the upper hand or they wouldn't be skulking around Lampura questioning people like that."

"Will they release him?"

"If everything goes as planned."

"Tell me." She gripped his shirt.

She'd promised herself she'd keep a tight rein on her emotions. She'd taken a risk back there, one that threatened both their lives if she'd been wrong. But if anything had happened to Nick, anything, her life wouldn't have been worth living.

Connie hated clichés. Modern love was supposed to be an exercise in equality, independence. Dying a little every time someone you loved was hurt wasn't supposed to happen anymore. Connie had to look no further than her mother's slow withering to know that people did die of broken hearts. Deprived of someone you loved completely, life quickly lost its meaning.

Which is why it was so important to her that her father know she was looking for him, that she hadn't given up.

And that Nick know how desperate she'd been to stop those men from hurting him. Not for the first time in her life, she put her own happiness on hold. Contacting the rebels had reinforced her need to save her father. She had to concentrate on him for the time being.

Nick carefully took her hands from his shirt. "The idea is to exchange him for another prisoner."

Connie's heart tripped. "When?"

"I don't have all the particulars. You'll have to prepare yourself for this." Deep down, Nick wondered if anyone ever could, if he was spinning her fairy tales when he should be telling her over and over again how much he loved her. "He may be changed. He may be bitter or just plain broken. You won't know until you see him."

"Oh, Nick."

He took her face in his hands, sifting his fingers through her cinnamon-colored hair and watching the afternoon sun glint off it, as if he held fire in his hands. Could he hold on to even one of those flames to light all the dark nights to come?

She wanted her father more than she wanted him. It was idiotic to expect a woman to make a choice like that—a lover or a father. And that's why he'd made the choice for her. He was going to save her father the only way no one had tried so far, by exchanging himself for Bill Hennessy. There'd be no happily-ever-afters. Connie had given him a chance to redeem himself, to do one idealistic, courageous act that might lose her to him, but would cement him in her heart forever.

He kissed her cheek. He meant to be gentle, but in seconds he'd found her mouth and speared her with a kiss meant for keeping.

"Nick. I don't know what I would have done if they'd taken you away from me."

"Don't think about it."

"I have to. They hit you. Let me see."

She unbuttoned his shirt with fumbling fingers. "Take this off. I want to look at your shoulder."

It ached bone-deep. Nick didn't care. All he knew was, he couldn't have shrugged his shirt off if he tried and Connie's mouth was the shade of those flowers on the balcony.

"Don't," she said breathlessly.

He lifted his lips from hers and smiled. "I've never known you to be so eager to undress me."

"Atwell, I want to nurse you."

He ran the backs of his fingers across her breast. "I'll keep that in mind."

She grimaced and gave up on the shoulder blade. Frowning, she searched out the other injury, unbuttoning his shirt until the buckle on his narrow belt stopped her. She tugged the shirt free and popped the last buttons.

A ridge of well-defined muscle rippled at her touch; a blue bruise showed through.

"Knocked the wind out of me, that's all," he insisted, not wanting to see the pain on her face. "It'll be gone by tomorrow."

Her eyes filled with tears she had no energy to suppress. Some people would see them as a sign of weakness. She knew they revealed the true strength of her feelings. "You could have been— I had to stop them, Nick. If anything happened to you—"

He wrapped her in his arms, his chin resting on the top of her head. "If anything *had* happened, you'd go straight to George at the embassy. Got that? He'd sort it all out. Just remember, your father is your main concern. Always was."

She shook her head. "You're in this, too, Nick. I love you."

He kissed her slow and deep because that's what she needed—because that's what he'd remember. He gripped her waist and held her to him, his bared chest sliding against the wilted silk of her blouse, the soft give of her breasts. "Remember what I said. No matter what happens, I love you."

"Promise me we won't lose each other."

He didn't look at her that time. He nipped the side of her neck and felt her knees bump his. "You'll have your father back."

"I want you."

"We can't always have what we want." He clenched his jaw at the sharpness in his voice, the tension he read in her body. "If I could give you everything you wanted, believe me I would. I just don't see how."

She stepped away from him, wriggling out of his

grip because she couldn't think when he held her like that, when his breath feathered over her skin, hot and humid like the fragrance of those flowers, making her sink into his arms and forget everything but the two of them. "I love my father, Nick. It's up to me to save him."

"And me."

"That doesn't mean I love you less." If anything, it meant more. She loved the man who was going to give her her father back. She loved his determination, his self-effacing courage. Dammit, she loved his style. Standing in the middle of this grimy hotel room, his shirt opened, his hair in total disarray, a black lock playing truant on his forehead, he still looked as suave as Cary Grant, as unflappable as Ronald Colman.

He hid his hurts well.

Not from her. Her father was almost free, and Nick was trying to distance himself from her. "You want me to leave with him and not look back."

"It'd be for the best."

She spit out a pithy British expletive telling him exactly what he could do with "the best." "It's the *possible* I'm thinking about. We can make this work, Nick. I can come back as soon as my father is well and settled in America. You could get transferred."

"I doubt I'm going anywhere soon. The Foreign Office has made it very clear what they think of me."

"They don't know what you're capable of."

Very true, Nick thought. He ran a hand through his hair, raising his arm to do it. A grunt of pain escaped him. "Let's not argue this now."

"We have to. If the rebels are here, if the government is going to fall, things could happen very fast."

"That's enough excitement for today. As I recall, we had a very long night."

She stood in the center of the room, her arms hanging at her sides. "Why don't you trust me?"

He turned, pain cutting through him. "I love you

more than I can possibly say. More than you'd ever believe even if I could say it. I can give you only so much, Connie. You'll have to forgive me if it isn't everything you want."

"How can you say that?"

He tilted his head and tried to think of a better way of putting it, but his mind had turned to mush. He walked into the bathroom. "Order us up some dinner, will you, love? I'll only be a moment."

Connie listened to the shower, her shower. He meant to take one here, to eat here and, she prayed, to sleep here. As long as he stayed, she could let the argument go, for now.

Connie walked over to the phone to dial the one-digit number for room service. By the time she worked the order out with the Lampuran cook, she wasn't sure what dishes would arrive and when. It didn't matter. Nick was here. If she had her way, he wouldn't leave until morning. That gave her one night to convince him to stay the rest of her life.

And if it didn't work? She sat on the edge of the bed and tried to convince herself she'd ask for no more. No future, no rose-covered cottages. No daydreams, no illusions. She couldn't predict the future any more than he could deny it.

Never let a chance slip away to tell someone you love them, she thought. He had the idea her father was *all* she cared about. When he finished with that shower, she'd show him different.

The rustling at the door woke Nick. Connie slept in the crook of his arm. Her breath stirred tiny hairs on his chest, bringing his right nipple to a lazy peak.

He listened intently in the dark. A whisper of paper slipped underneath the door. Nick made out the triangle of white in the moonlight.

They'd made love until little more than an hour before, then dozed off. He hoped Connie would sleep until morning. The tears following their last love-making proved how wrought up she still was, her emotions teetering between elation over her father's possible release and terror at what might have happened to them today.

And sorrow at the future they could envision for themselves.

Nick's tension eased as the footsteps receded down the hallway. Whoever it was had left only the note. They'd expect no one to find it until morning. Nick would see to it in a minute, as soon as he kissed Connie's hair, stroking her shoulder with the very edges of his fingertips, loving her every way he knew how without waking her.

He hadn't been gentleman enough to bow out gracefully after taking that shower. In actual fact, he hadn't had time to bow out. She'd joined him, sliding back the curtain rings and stepping in beside him, naked, tendrils of her hair circling her breasts like parentheses.

When he'd touched her, she'd thrown her head back and let the water wash down her throat, followed quickly by his lips. She'd laughed, his sea goddess. He'd lifted her against the wall and felt her legs clench at his waist, her arms grip his neck.

A ledge waist-high ringed the shower stall. He'd balanced her hips against it, splaying his hands on the wall beside her as he thrust into her. She'd been ready for him, molten and slick.

She'd come apart in his arms, clutching him to her, calling his name. His mouth had gone taut, his body sinewy and tense. He reared back. She'd watched the strain on his face, a trickle of sweat meandering down his temple, mingling with the glisten of water.

They'd watched together, gazes trailing downward, moving and joining in a rhythm that could have been dictated by the sea, the hushed pulse of a pounding wave rushing to shore, until they erupted together, like a volcano. Her nails dented his back where the bruise was; he didn't care. Pain was part of it, another sensation sharp and sweet.

He wanted it to remind him nothing was perfect, nothing. Not idealism, not optimism. Only love was strong enough to see him through what he had to do. This woman gave him that strength, recalling him to a life he'd thought buried beneath a questionable reputation.

She'd given him everything—instinctive trust, unwarranted faith, unearned love. He'd earn it with her father's freedom. If he was lucky, she'd forgive him. Staring up at the fan whose blades hadn't moved since the shelling of the power station four nights ago, Nick wondered if he'd ever find out.

He sighed and reviewed his plan. After he exchanged himself for Bill Hennessy, he could negotiate his own release. Maybe. Any way he looked at it, he'd have plenty of time to talk. Perhaps years.

"Are you awake?"

Nick's heart clutched in his chest. "Evening, love."

"It isn't morning?"

He tilted his head toward the moon. "Not for hours."

"Are you leaving?"

"Not for hours."

She smiled a sleepy, pleased smile. "What are you thinking?"

"That I love you." He kept his voice light, teasing. "Isn't that what one is supposed to say at a time like this?"

She poked his ribs. "I knew that much."

"Did you?"

"Never doubted it."

He kissed her hair and slipped his arm out from under her head, substituting a pillow before he sat up. "You believed in me from the first. I never did find out why."

She shrugged, the sheet's edge skimming over her

breasts. "One learns to size people up quickly when asking for favors."

"You saw through me, eh?"

"All the way to your idealism." She ran a fingernail down his spine, making him stiffen.

He stared at the triangle of paper under the door. A corner of it stuck out in the hallway. He'd have to get up and get it before someone walked by and filched it. "You expecting any mail?"

"Hmm?"

Nick walked naked to the door. He unfolded the paper and stepped over by the open window to read by the moonlight. "*Your package has arrived, all one hundred eighty pounds of it. Room 241.*" No name. No other comment.

Nick pondered it a moment.

"What is it?" Connie asked.

"A communiqué."

"For me?"

"I don't think so." That's what was so curious about it.

Paul Bianca, Connie's ex-husband, had wired Nick two days ago that he'd be in Lampura as soon as he got leave from the Navy. Fortunately, his ship had been in Japan and the journey wasn't far. Obviously, the "package" was him.

Just as obviously, someone intended this note for Nick. Who knew Nick was here? Who suspected? And why did that handwriting ring a bell? "Why, George, you sly devil."

"Is that who wrote it?" Connie slipped up beside him.

Nick folded the note over and put an arm around her shoulders. Perhaps Bianca had reported to the embassy when he'd arrived and George Cunningham had put two and two together. As for knowing where to find Nick, only George would be this sure. "Without ever leaving that embassy, George knows as much about Lampura as I do. He sees through everyone."

"Then why doesn't he promote you off this island?"

"I'll have to ask him that myself sometime."

Connie swatted his backside."You do that. Now come back to bed."

Nick obeyed.

"So how does he know so much?" Connie asked. She covered her mouth for a yawn, her curiosity rapidly losing a battle with fatigue.

"One of life's mysteries."

"Ask him."

Nick chuckled at Connie's straightforward American approach. "The man could say no to the Queen herself. Tactfully, of course."

"You going to answer his note?"

"In the morning."

Nick rested his head against the wall. If events developed the way he hoped, there'd be no more nights like this, no more dawns.

Lovemaking couldn't last forever. Only memories. Her father had lived on them for a decade. Nick would too. But first, selfishly, he had to make more, to make the kind of love that created the memories he'd need where he was going.

He took her in his arms, determined to love her enough this final time, to last a lifetime. Their passion would slow the dawn and forestall the sun.

Nine

Connie was sure her body had never been more thoroughly loved, nor her emotions so stimulated. Her world had changed. For years the focus had been her father and his freedom. Yet here on this little island, she'd found love. Could a heart really accommodate two emotions this big?

Could Nick really think she'd let him go after sharing them? Saving one man had been her goal for half her life, loving Nick became her goal for the rest of it. "Nick."

"Mm?" Sitting at the desk in her hotel room, he continued writing a hasty note as the sun came up.

"Nothing," she said. She hadn't meant to say his name aloud. Just as she didn't mean to tell him one simple truth: She never gave up when she knew she was right. If Nick didn't know it, he'd soon find out.

The red morning haze tinted the room, outlining his back in a hot glow as he crumpled a sheet of hotel stationery and rustled another out of the drawer.

He curled his toes when he wrote, she noted with a smile, long angular toes, bony ankles. He wore slacks but no shirt, the bruises clearly marked on his glistening skin. Occasionally he slicked his hair back with one hand, holding a wayward lock off his forehead where it threatened to come down and interrupt his concentration.

"A note to George," he muttered aloud, aware of her loving gaze lingering on him.

"In code?"

"Just tough to write."

"About my father?"

"Yes." He looked up at last. "He'll be all right, Con."

She smiled a thank you. Nick couldn't make promises, they both knew that. It was kind of him to try. "What will happen exactly?"

"No telling, exactly. The idea is, we trade him for another hostage, one the rebels will believe more valuable."

"I'm not sure I like the idea of trading in human beings."

Nick appraised her for a long time. Then he came over and lifted her chin with his fingertips. "You are one fantastic woman, you know that?"

"This other man will have a family too. There must be people who care about him."

Nick told himself to let go. Let go now. Walk away and finish that damned letter. Instead he sat beside her, wrapping her in his arms until he was sure she'd guess, she'd know. "Maybe they'll be proud of him."

"He won't have much choice, will he? I mean, not if he's a prisoner."

A prisoner of love, Nick thought, a wry smile on his face. The flash of humor deserted him as quickly as it had come. He had to tell her somehow. Kisses were too vague, too easy, too satisfying. Like caresses, they spoke volumes and never said enough.

He returned to the desk. "Your father's more important right now."

"To me he is."

Truer words were never spoken, Nick thought. He crumpled this letter too. Inadequate, stilted. The only way he could free her father was to substitute himself. Why pretend she'd understand that? He'd maneuvered himself into a corner of his own making, breaking her heart in order to show her how much he loved her. There was no way out now. What a queer reversal of tradition. Instead of her father giving Nick his daughter's hand, Nick was giving her her father's. He loved her that much.

The paper in front of him remained blank.

"You know what I think?" she asked from the bed.

"Mmm?"

"That you and I, together, can handle just about anything. Rebels disguised as government soldiers, balky plumbing in lukewarm showers. Whitcraft."

He laughed mirthlessly.

"It's amazing how two people can find each other from opposite sides of the globe and be so alike."

"How is that?"

Her milky shoulder raised and lowered in a feline shrug. She switched her hair off it, the cinnamon coloring echoing the faint freckles scattered there. "We both have to hide our real beliefs, tailoring what we say, negotiating. But underneath it, we believe in loyalty and sacrifice."

Believe in us, Connie wanted to say. "Heck, if we can save a man who's been held hostage for ten years, we can work out a relationship. People do that every day."

"In the regular world, yes."

"What's so different about this one?"

Nick scrawled the last of his letter and signed his name. "In the real world, people have some say in their future. When you're father's free, you'll be able to go anywhere, start over, meet people, date in earnest, maybe marry someone. In the real world, we wouldn't have met."

"But we did."

"Do you ever think of remarrying?" He was trying to change the subject.

"I thought of it last night," Connie answered.

Nick put the note in an envelope. "I meant remarrying Paul. You said you parted friends. Maybe you two could get back together."

She laughed tenderly at his matchmaking. "And where would you be?"

"Here."

"Don't look so grim. People get transferred. You could even quit, get a different kind of job."

"Where else can a man decipher code for a living?"

Connie wrinkled her nose. "You like that?"

"Very much."

"So why are you doing all this other stuff?"

"It'd be selfish of me to get a comfortable desk job when so many countries are tearing themselves apart."

Connie sauntered over, ignoring the open window despite her nakedness. "You don't have to save them all." She wrapped her arms around Nick from the back and squeezed.

He sealed the envelope. "I haven't saved anyone up to now. I'd feel I'd failed if I quit without making some mark." He'd just never dreamed the price of success would be this high. He closed his eyes and let her kiss him on each temple.

"You've helped *me*, Nick. Immeasurably."

His hands shook when she nipped the side of his neck like that. "Glad to be of service." The graininess ran deeper than his usual morning voice.

Connie didn't question how she knew that. She cherished the fact she did, treasuring those things only lovers knew, people who had a lifetime before them to run up whole lists of little taken-for-granted things. How he liked his coffee, how he fidgeted when he was trying to concentrate. How he kissed.

The way he evaded taking credit for things anyone else would expect a medal for. How she loved him at this particular moment.

She could almost love Lampura right now, a tropical paradise, an Eden for two. Her doubts grew as faint as the last indigo blue of the night sky, until at last they vanished, replaced by something passionate, warm as the morning sun.

He looked at her. So beautiful. *Paul will hold you when I'm gone,* Nick thought. *He'll take you away from here.* If, afterward, Connie turned to her ex-husband in despair and was comforted, did Nick have any right to resent it? He did. He did.

Connie kissed the pulse in the side of his jaw. "Even if you couldn't save my father, I'd still love you. Anyway, you got me off the subject." She plopped herself down on his lap. "I'm a pushy broad when I have to be. And you're tactful and bite your tongue when you absolutely have to. Underneath it all, I think we want the same things."

"New lives?"

"One life. Together." Connie had never dreamed of proposing to a man. But at times like this, the conventions ceased to matter. She wanted a promise from him before all hell broke loose, before she saw her father again. She needed Nick beside her, she'd needed him from the first. "Well?"

He ran his palm over the desk top, as if memorizing the grain of the wood, the slant of the light. Then he shifted his fingers to her thigh, tracing the slope of pearly skin until rivulets of heat shimmered deep inside her. "You rescued us from the rebels yesterday. I'd say you handled that perfectly."

"See what a great wife you'd be getting?"

"I saw a woman who can survive without me."

She nudged his temple with her nose, planting quick kisses there. "A woman who doesn't want to."

So clear-eyed, Nick thought. So to-the-point. How

could he lie to her while cradling her on his lap? How could a hand cover a woman's breast and not communicate too much? Try as he might, he couldn't let go. And he couldn't let her see the conflicting emotions drawing his mouth into a frown beyond his control, binding his chest so tautly, his heart hurt.

He cleared his throat. "Have I told you how very proud I am of you? I don't know what gives me the right to say that. The first day I saw you, I thought a man would be honored to have your love. A man would do just about anything to earn it."

"Including marrying me?"

"I wanted to tell you that last night. We never got around to it."

She playfully wrapped her arms around his neck. "All you told me last night was that you loved me and that you wanted me to put my hand here"—she demonstrated—"and that I should never ever forget you. Do you really think that's possible?"

Nick wasn't sure swallowing was possible, considering what she did to him. "Darling, it's almost day. We've got things to see to."

He'd thought that would bring her back to reality. Instead, her eyes grew smoky and her voice rough. "Don't go yet. Please. I need to know what happens next. I have this crazy feeling that saving him will mean losing you."

Nick understood completely. It wasn't sex. She wanted to seize the few hours they had left, just as he had last night.

Foolishly, romantically, he found himself pressing the back of her hand to his lips, just as he'd wished to do that day at the embassy. He stood and set her on her feet, the bandages there reduced to two thin strips. "Meet me in the restaurant downstairs in an hour."

He tugged on his shirt so quickly Connie could barely formulate her question before the door shut behind him. "Does this mean no to my proposal?" she called after him.

"It means good-bye. For now."

Connie tried to laugh in the silent room. "So much for commitment." He hadn't given her an answer. She saw that clearly enough. But she wasn't letting it bother her. Not a bit. The man loved her. She loved him. He saw too many angles, too many political problems in their way. He didn't see what a woman in love could do. An invigorating sense of optimism and hope refused to let her down. That was love. It could resolve any problems, last years, and stretch across continents.

On a more mundane note, Nick hadn't said whether they were going to the mountains or a tea with the Premier. She had to find an outfit to wear. Lampura had two seasons, wet hot days and dry hot days. And one day when her father's captivity would end. Could it be today?

"One man at a time," Connie reminded herself. Turning on the shower, she set her watch on the basin so she wouldn't be late. She thought about a lot of things under the drizzling spray: how love turned duty into a privilege, how people surprised themselves by rising above difficulties they never expected to face. And what a good man Nick Atwell was!

Her father would like him. "I love him, Dad."

She put the final touches on her hair, inserting the diamond stud earrings her father had given her mother on their wedding day. Wearing a go-any-where outfit of loose pleated slacks and a white blouse scalloped in a heart-shaped neckline, she glanced around for her purse. In his haste to scurry away, Nick had inadvertently left his note behind, and he'd forgotten to put George's name on the envelope. She was tempted to leave it where it was and tell Nick to come back for it.

"Connie Hennessy, that is the lowest form of feminine subterfuge! Chase a man off with a marriage proposal then lure him back with lost items. You'll be in politics next."

She tucked the letter in her purse, then headed for the restaurant and a rendezvous with the man she loved.

"Something cooking?"

Nick spun around, a hand halfway through his hair, his tie askew, and his handkerchief clutched in his fist. "George!"

"Touchy today."

Aside from the wry comment, George Cunningham gave no indication of noticing Nick's attack of nerves. He helped himself to a seat across from Nick's desk and began musing aloud, George's favorite form of communication. "Too many goings on around here lately."

"Yes," Nick said. Where was that damn note? He couldn't have left it in Connie's room. If she read it now, everything would be ruined. She'd never let him go over to the rebels of his own accord.

Isn't that what you wanted, his conscience chimed, *for her never to let you go?*

Not if it meant scenes and tears and heartbreaking good-byes. She needed to start over, elsewhere, living a decent, normal life with a husband who could provide for her and a father whose predicament no longer haunted her days.

George's calm recital of the known facts of the recent rebel attack interrupted Nick's fidgeting. "Lose something?"

"Only my mind," Nick said, a sick smile canting his mouth. "What else is new?"

George could shrug while giving the impression of never moving a muscle. "I would have said your heart, old boy."

Nick gave him a long flat look. *Dodge*, his mind whispered fiercely, *laugh it off, lie, do something*. Instead he stared, a man who'd lost every ability he'd ever had to pretend something he didn't feel. "Is it that obvious?"

"More obvious than what you plan to do about it."

For a moment Nick had the sinking sensation George knew that too. "What do you mean?"

"You've been all over town."

"Squiring Miss Hennessy. My mission was to keep her out of Whitcraft's hair, as I recall."

"And how do you expect to do that if you don't secure her father's release? She's not going anywhere, is she?"

"No."

"Then the airline tickets for three in the name of Paul Bianca aren't for her, her father, and you?"

Nick cursed silently, his face a mask of civility. "Didn't know you were an enemy, George."

"My dear boy, you wound me."

"Not the way I will if you try to stop me."

George trailed a finger across his upper lip. "Desperadoes, now, are we?"

Nick laughed, a dry husky sound. This wasn't like him at all. "I apologize, George. A little tense. I didn't mean to threaten you."

"Relieved to hear it. About this Bianca character who stopped by looking for you."

"Connie's ex-husband. An expert in terrorist countertactics."

"The Navy SEALs, yes, he mentioned that. Go anywhere, do anything."

"Rambo in a wetsuit."

"Our American cousins are something, aren't they?"

"I talked to him this morning before I left the hotel. He'll help you get her off the island when her father is free."

"So she leaves with Bianca and her father and you stay behind. Final scene of *Casablanca*, eh?"

"Something like that."

"Or *A Tale of Two Cities*? 'It is a far, far better thing—'" George stopped his recitation the moment he saw the shadow cross Nick's face. The pen Nick had picked up tocked against the desk top. "Have you thought this through, Nicholas?"

"It will get him out."

"And put you in."

"I'd be a renegade."

"Her Majesty's government does not negotiate with terrorists, you know that."

"But *they* don't. The rebels believe a diplomat from Britain will be more valuable than an aging American doctor."

In the silence, both men thought about what could happen when the rebels found out that wasn't true.

George stood up. With his slightly puffy middle-aged appearance, he could pass for anything from forty to sixty. Nick thought he looked sixty now.

"You know, of all the staff, I've always had the highest opinion of you."

"Put that in my personnel file."

"Tut tut. You're far too valuable to go respectable. You're undercover in your own office. Why, with your contacts— But you didn't honestly think you were out on a limb all this time?"

His elbows balanced on the ledge of his desk, his hands clasped, Nick looked up at George and nodded. The man looked even older.

"There are people—" George paused, at a loss for soothing and appropriate words for the first time in all the years Nick had known him, and with more suppressed feeling than Nick had ever heard. "There *are* people here who appreciate all you've done."

"Thank you, George. Look, I've written a letter, a note really. If Connie comes here with it . . . See to it she's taken care of, will you?"

"I'll have to alert the ambassador to your actions, you know. Eventually."

Nick laughed.

"Good-bye, Nick."

"Good-bye, George."

"Paul!"

Paul Bianca's customary bear hug cut off Connie's delighted exclamation. He whirled her around the restaurant of the Imperial Hotel and gamely set her on her feet. "How's my girl?"

"Fine, but what are you—"

"Line of work, remember?" He tapped her on the nose.

Looking up at the stocky rough-and-tumble man with the crew cut, Connie recalled their code. That tap meant don't be nosy. She remembered other things, how protected she'd always felt with Paul, how scrappy he was, how decent.

"No guilt," he commanded. "You always give me that guilty look."

"Like when?"

"On the courthouse steps, for one. I said it was okay, remember?"

"Your being such a great guy didn't make it any easier for me to divorce you. How are you?"

"Fine. You're looking gorgeous. Considering."

He meant her father; their conversations always returned to that. His captivity had brought them together and broken them apart. How would his freedom change things between her and Nick? Connie squeezed Paul's hand until she feared her nails would make permanent marks. He let her.

"Want to sit down?"

"Before I fall down," she sighed.

She'd prepared herself for a day of unknowns by concentrating on one thing only, breakfast with Nick. However, waiting half an hour hadn't been part of the bargain. After twenty minutes her nerves won out, and she'd been a wreck of anticipation and apprehension.

Its shattered windows boarded over since the rebel attack, the restaurant was dimmer than usual. Paul escorted her to a candlelit booth. Maybe catching up with him would keep her nerves in check until Nick arrived. She'd swiveled her neck to that archway so often, she'd developed a creak.

Paul sat with his back to the wall, as always.

Connie smiled fondly and reached for his hand. "I know you won't say anything you shouldn't, but I can make some inferences as to why you're here."

"Such as?" He snapped a napkin open and spread it on his lap.

"Well, the less you say, the more important it has to be. Maybe America is making its presence felt on Lampura again. Maybe you're scouting out the rebel's chances of winning. Maybe—" she took a sip of water, her hand shaking, "maybe a rescue attempt is in the works."

Maybe, Connie thought, her heart hammering, that was part of the plan Nick hadn't explained yet.

Paul shook his head. "I'm here on my own. Thought you might need me."

"But how did you know? Why here, why now?"

"Got a call. Sources behind the scenes."

"On whose side?"

"On your side, babe. As for me, I'm serving in a completely neutral capacity."

"You sound like Nick now."

"Nick?"

The careful way he said that one word made her skin prickle. She supposed it was natural for a former husband to be a bit wary of another man— and entirely natural for Paul to be overly protective. She bit her lip. The secret couldn't keep forever. "I'm thinking of getting married again."

"Yeah?" To her surprise, he looked genuinely pleased. "Who to?"

"A diplomat here on the island. Nick Atwell."

Paul's smile stayed in place, but the light in his eyes faded to an opaque gray she'd never been able to read or penetrate. "The one who's helping you," he said flatly.

"Please don't be jealous."

"Who said I was?"

"I'm not making the mistake I made with you. I'm still sorry about that, but I think this is the real thing."

The more sincerely she gazed in his eyes, the less pleased he looked.

Paul could say a lot by saying nothing for minutes on end.

"How well do you know this guy?" he asked at last.

She pulled her shoulders back. "Very well." Enduring Paul's searching look, she almost qualified that. "I'm sure you'll like him when you meet him."

"I have. He stopped by my room this morning. Somehow I got the impression he'd just left yours."

"I'm a grown woman, Paul."

"Maybe I just don't like what he's doing to you."

"That's not really any of your business."

"Then why am I here? And where is he?"

Connie had managed all of three minutes without glancing at the entrance. "I don't know. I'm in such a state, I get paranoid if I don't see him for fifteen minutes. After what happened with father, I'm afraid of losing anyone I love too much."

"And that's exactly what he's doing!" Paul grabbed her hand, muttering expletives only a Navy man would know. "We're outta here."

"Don't you dare drag me out of a public restaurant! What are you doing?"

"Excuse me, are you bothering this woman?" Nick

appeared under the archway, casually swiping a palm frond away from his face.

"About time you showed up," Paul said. "Thought you'd gone off on some hot-dogging expedition of your own."

Nick looked mildly shocked at the rebuke.

"Guess you two have met," Connie muttered, totally exasperated with both of them. The last thing she needed was playing referee to two male egos. "Will someone please tell me what's going on?"

Nick patted his brow with his handkerchief and prodded it back into his pocket, looking as disheveled and rakish as ever. And yet, he couldn't hide a keenness every time he glanced at her. "Meeting at the embassy ran a little late. Sorry, darling." He gave her a polite peck on the cheek.

Connie took a step back, the better to look them both up and down while her eyes narrowed. "Don't give me that. You're both up to something."

"The curse of an intelligent wife," Paul whispered to Nick.

Nick plunged his hands into his pockets and jangled some change. "A long search for a short letter. You haven't seen it by any chance?"

Connie reached into her purse and presented it. "Don't sidetrack me with trifles, Atwell. Spill it."

Nick turned the envelope over in his hands. For a second Connie thought he was checking to see if she'd opened it. Another way of sidetracking her from the main issue, no doubt. "Imagine running into my ex like this?" she purred.

Nick smiled, the soul of politeness. "It's a small, small world."

"Getting smaller by the minute."

"Kinda like your shorts, buddy." Paul gave Nick a dig with his elbow.

Nick raised his eyebrows in earnest. "I beg your pardon?"

"He means you're in trouble, Nick."

"Ah. Did I say something wrong?"

"You never say anything wrong," she said. "You set up this little rendezvous and I want to know why."

Paul leaned over to Nick. "I love her when she's tough, don't you?"

Nick nodded, but said nothing. He seemed content to memorize her face.

Paul grinned, mistaking that gaze for stubborn silence. "I think you've met your match, babe."

"Don't call me babe. And don't you freeze me out, Atwell. Why is Paul here?"

"He hasn't said?"

"You could pull out his fingernails and he wouldn't say. He's trained that way."

"And you think I'm trained to give honest answers? I could make something up."

Connie crossed her arms. "Nice try, but no one's getting out of here until I'm satisfied. Something's up and I have a right to know."

Nick and Paul traded looks, silently conferring on the wisdom of outwitting a five-foot-seven-inch Hennessy when she dug her heels in. At a nod from Paul, Nick answered. "I'm sure your former husband only wishes to give you what support he can in this time of trouble."

Connie snorted. Not a flicker of guilt between them. They could stand there all day, like trees. She threw up her hands. "Just my luck to get saddled with an unflappable Englishman and a close-mouthed American!"

Paul raised a callused hand. "Take this out on *him*, I just got here."

Connie dearly wanted to, almost as badly as she wanted to clasp Nick in her arms and hold on for dear life. Frustration and tension warred inside her. How could she say any of that when he stood there as cool and collected as if this were any ordinary Tuesday?

He still hadn't answered her question from this morning. She'd hoped they'd have time to talk over brunch. Did he want to marry her? Did he see any future for them at all? "I wanted to talk to you."

"I'll explain in the car."

Ten

Nick stopped the Land Rover on the edge of the clearing and smiled grimly to himself. They were doing exactly what he'd warned Connie not to do—drive off into the mountains to deal with the rebels. The only difference was the Land Rover he'd borrowed from the embassy garage. It would carry Paul, Connie, and her father to Lampura City. They'd be traveling fast over rutted roads. Without him.

The ride up had been silent for the most part, the scenery overgrown and oppressive. Love and apprehension tangled in Nick like briars in a rosebush. His determination overcame them all.

Somewhere a bird shrieked. Nick's heartbeat leveled off to a manageable thud. If anyone asked, he'd blame his sweat-soaked hands on the heat.

Obviously, Connie hadn't guessed his intentions. She'd be arguing with him if she had, pleading, doing everything she'd done in Whitcraft's office that first day but with considerably more passion. That's the kind of woman she was, seeing right through him to the honorable, idealistic core that had never entirely withered and died. She'd provoked him into reviving what was best in him, living up to *her* image of what he could be.

She'd probably hate him for it.

A trickle of fear ran between his shoulder blades. He took a deep business-as-usual breath and grinned at his passengers. Paul wasn't fooled, he knew the plan. Connie was absorbed in staring at the empty clearing.

"Will he come from over there?" she asked.

"They may not even show up," Paul interrupted bluntly.

He'd been giving Nick black looks ever since they'd departed the Imperial Hotel. Nick wondered why. When they'd met that morning in his hotel room, Paul had said he was impressed with Nick's plan, not to mention his courage. For the last hour the man had treated Nick as if he'd given Connie a social disease.

"Shall we step out?" Nick suggested. "They may be waiting to see we're unarmed and alone."

Towering foliage muffled the sound of the Land Rover's doors opening and shutting. A blanket of humidity cloaked the jungle. Nevertheless, Nick couldn't help noticing the way Connie rubbed her arms as if chilled.

She took a few steps forward, wiping her palms on her pleated slacks before spreading her hands to demonstrate her defenselessness to any silent observers.

His heart full, Nick watched her. There was no way to stop her coming all the way to the center of the clearing with him. She'd made that plain as he'd explained the procedure to her on the tense ride up.

"He's *my* father," she'd said. "I'm not standing on the sidelines while you do this, Nick."

"The Colonel might not like that," he murmured.

"He's met me."

"And I dare say he was favorably impressed."

She gave him one of her don't-play-diplomat-with-me looks.

"What if he sends seconds?" Nick tried. It'd be so much easier if she stayed by the car. Otherwise she might notice him hanging back, remaining behind. "They could scatter at the least deviation from the plan."

"Then tell me the plan," she demanded.

Nick sketched it in. "I assume we'll be ringed by rebels out of sight in the forest. When I walk into the clearing, they'll bring your father out and we'll make the exchange."

"Who's bringing the prisoner *we're* exchanging? Won't they be suspicious if the government people show up late?"

"No." He refrained from answering in any more detail. "We show up alone. Then the exchange. Then back down the mountain as fast as possible. I stopped by your hotel room before going to the restaurant—" Searching frantically for that note, he didn't add. "I threw your clothes in a case. Not the neatest arrangement, but it'll help you clear out fast. The plane leaves at four."

"I know when the plane leaves," she said. "You're trying to get rid of me."

"I'm trying to get you and your father to safety. Paul has agreed to help."

Nick wanted to believe he could argue that stubborn tilt out of her chin. With a few more days, he might even have convinced her his plan was sound. He didn't have time.

Paul had reached over the back seat and put a hand on Connie's shoulder. "It'll be okay."

"I know." Her eye caught Nick's as he downshifted on a tight curve. She placed one hand on Paul's and the other on Nick's arm. "I'm lucky to have both of you helping me. Thanks for coming, Paul."

Back in the clearing, Paul signaled Nick from the tail end of the Rover.

"You know, I can fade into these trees, circle around, see what I can do."

Nick appreciated the man's skills sight unseen; the SEALs were legendary in direct proportion to the secrecy surrounding their deeds. "Thanks, Paul, but you know your role."

"Get 'em out of here."

"Yes."

"And not wait for you."

Nick nodded.

"She could've done worse. Still, I don't like it."

"We can't all have your training. Twenty men like you—"

Paul snorted. "Six might've done it if the mission had ever been authorized. What I meant was, she loves you and you're going to break her heart."

That had always been the flaw in the plan. "It's better this way."

"Have you asked her about that?"

"It's the most I can give her."

"Hey, I had no problem with it until I saw how it was with you two."

"Then tell her," Nick said, his teeth clenched. He tugged the knot in his tie. "When you get her on that plane, tell her I'm as worthless as I always claimed. Tell her there's nothing to come back for. For the first time since she turned sixteen, she'll be free to choose her own life without any of this hanging over her head. Make her see that."

"And if she wants you?"

Nick watched Connie standing in the clearing. Her shoulders straightened, her back stiffened. He made out the figures moving through the trees at the same time she did. She whirled to him, pleading in her eyes. He went to her, Paul's question taunting him. *What if she wants you?*

Connie put her hand out to Nick and squeezed as hard as she could. She wasn't sure her lungs could deal with this dead air, the smothering heat. She'd been strong so long, she couldn't fall apart now. "Mom worked so hard . . ."

He put an arm around her shoulder. Someone spoke a warning from the shadowy trees. Nick withdrew and stepped away from her. The back of his hand brushed hers.

Soldiers appeared in their mixed and matched uniforms, khaki and mottled forest green and the dull shine of guns. Between two of them a tall man in a wrinkled white shirt staggered into the clearing.

Connie's heart lodged in her throat. Her hand flew to her mouth to stifle a cry.

Nick squeezed her hand. "Do exactly as I say. Promise me."

She nodded, never taking her eyes off the gaunt old man.

Dr. Hennessy saw them. He stopped and bent over, as if a pain tore through him. Connie felt that pain. Then his head rose, his shoulders squared. With a dignified, steady gait he came toward them, towering over the soldiers on either side of him, trailed by the bald man Nick called the Colonel.

Her father's shirt was similar to the Colonel's, tailless, untucked. Broad but bony American shoulders filled out the shapelessness. At first Connie had thought he looked old, but the nearer he drew, the younger he appeared, until, with a faint smile and a nod her way, she saw the man she'd never forgotten.

Her fears vanished. How could she have imagined him a ruin, when only a very strong man could have endured the last ten years? "Daddy."

Over a distance of twenty feet, he heard her. "Hi, kid."

The soldiers hushed him. He didn't flinch. They stopped ten feet away.

"Is all prepared?" the Colonel asked in that peculiar metallic voice.

"Yes," Nick replied.

"You have your prisoner, we shall have ours."

Connie didn't see the government's prisoner any-where. She didn't care.

Nick nodded to the Colonel and stepped forward toward her father. With a lifetime's experience ob-serving the formalities, he extended his hand. "Good afternoon, sir. Nicholas Atwell. I can't tell you how pleased I am to meet you at last."

Her father smiled and shook his hand. "Same here. Call me Bill." The two men silently sized each other up. "Are you the one I should thank for all this?"

Connie could stand it no longer. She rushed for-ward and threw her arms around her father's waist.

He held her tight. "Here now."

Connie got control, letting go with one arm to reach for Nick's hand. "Yes, he's the one to thank, Dad. He's helped us so much."

"Your daughter is the real heroine here," Nick insisted.

Her father didn't miss Nick touching Connie's arm familiarly, protectively, the silent support of some-one who has a right to offer it.

His discerning look shouldn't have surprised her. Years of remembering his gentleness had obscured memories of his sharp intelligence. Her father had always read her like a book—whether she was sneaking out of the house or procrastinating on homework. He looked at her and Nick with that same clear-eyed evaluation.

"So," he said to Nick, "I hope you're taking care of her."

"You're our first concern, sir. Major Bianca there will take you to the city and a plane will have you on your way to Singapore within hours."

"The Americans are involved?"

"Paul's my ex-husband, Dad."

Her father looked past her to Paul, then back to Nick.

"I guess it's a long story," she laughed weakly.

"It's been a long time." A sudden weariness emphasized the lines around her father's eyes, as if every year away had been etched there. "You look just like your mother," he said.

Connie's eyes filled with tears. "Dad—"

He shook his head. "I know. I knew it when I saw she wasn't here. Maybe I've known it since they stopped giving me articles about her search."

"She never gave up. Never."

"Neither did you."

Behind them the Land Rover started. The soldiers fanned out. Nick glanced at the edge of the clearing. Paul hopped out of the vehicle and came toward them.

"Would you like us to bring round the car?" Nick asked, sensing the older man's fatigue.

"No. I'll walk it," Hennessy said. "It feels good to walk free." He let Connie support him as they began to move off. Paul came forward and took his other arm.

Connie twisted around to Nick. He waved her on. "I need a few words with the Colonel."

On some level Connie was aware of all of it, but nothing so specific as her father's ribs, the weight he'd lost, how willpower seemed to be the only thing holding him together.

"I'll get him to the car. Why don't you say good-bye," Paul offered.

Connie had no one to say good-bye to. She couldn't imagine speaking one civilized word to the Colonel. However, if Nick could manage it, maybe she could too. For his sake. The other hostage hadn't arrived yet. It might be wise to use up some time until he did.

She turned and came back. Ignoring Nick's dark look, she coolly slipped her arm around his waist and faced down the Colonel. "He looks all right," she said.

The bald man halted in the act of lighting one

cigarette from the ashes of another. "He's weathered his captivity well."

"No thanks to you." Connie felt Nick's back tense and bit her tongue.

The Colonel bowed, a feline smile creasing his face. "We have found ourselves a more valuable replacement. No offense to Dr. Hennessy."

"None taken," she said.

Nick drew her away a little. Murmured warnings in Lampuran halted him. "A minute," he asked.

"You have nothing but time," the evil little man replied.

Connie missed it. She missed every clue, every hint. She'd smiled up at Nick. "If I loved you any more, I'd bust. Thank you so much."

She got up on her toes to kiss him. To her surprise, he let her. With soldiers looking on, her father waiting, and Paul gunning the engine, she kissed Nick until the buzz of the insects and birds was drowned out by her own thudding heart, too full to put any of this in words. "Thank you."

He nodded.

She laughed. "Aren't you going to say something?"

He gazed into her eyes and shook his head. "Can't come up with a thing."

"Arranging all this must have taken some fancy talking. You'll have to tell me about it later." She stepped toward the Rover. "Coming?"

He shook his head, swallowed, took his handkerchief out of his pocket and gripped it in his hand. "I'm not done here."

"Hurry."

"Go ahead, Connie."

She turned in her tracks.

He strode toward her, three fast paces. Guns clicked. He didn't hear them. Before she knew what was happening, he swept her into his arms and kissed her breathless, a harsh, penetrating kiss that harbored no tact, no discretion, just passion and truth and things she couldn't put a name to.

He crammed the handkerchief into her hand. "Go."

"But—"

"Go."

Paul pulled up in the Rover. "Get in," he ordered.

A sudden paralyzing cold numbed her limbs. Moving like a zombie, she stumbled up the step as Paul gripped her arm. The noise of the jungle grew, shrieking and screaming in her ears, drowned out by the roaring of the Rover's engine as they took off.

"Wait," she cried, Nick's plan dawning on her at last, cutting through the one pure moment of elation she had allowed herself. Her father was free. They'd been home free!

It all shattered like glass. Her father, given a minute to talk to Paul alone, held her back with strength that astounded and enraged her. Paul gunned the Rover through the dense trees and onto the winding path. Nick disappeared behind a line of armed men.

Nick listened to the engine fade and wished the memory of Connie's cries would fade with it, the incoherent words, her too-coherent anguish, disbelief, fury.

A gun barrel swung around, pointing the way.

"At last I'll get to see where you hide yourselves," Nick said pleasantly.

"Not yet," the Colonel replied. With a flick of his cigarette he signaled for a blindfold.

The strip of scratchy black cloth stretched from Nick's forehead to his cheekbones, obliterating every trace of daylight. He clenched his teeth until a pulse in his jaw hammered. He hated darkness *and* confined spaces. Probably have plenty of both where he was going, he thought. But no use worrying now.

All the same, a clammy sensation crept along his skin.

Nick moved in the direction indicated by the gun barrel poking into his lower back. He tripped on aged koa-pora vines. No one helped him to his feet the second time.

"I realize it is an inconvenience," the bald man said. "You must bear with us."

A suitably disarming reply should have occurred to Nick, something along the lines of "I'm sure it is," or "Very wise." He should have kept the conversation flowing, put them at their ease, reassured them he was a reasonable man and they could negotiate with him. Nothing but ashes filled his mouth.

"You are very brave," the Colonel said a while later.

Nick pictured the man's bald head glinting less now that they'd entered the thickest part of the jungle. They were climbing, following a tortuous path up the side of a mountain. Half an hour back someone had pulled his hands behind him and cuffed him, making his balance that much harder to maintain. A dozen stumbles had torn the knees of his slacks. Blood caked one, making it stick to his skin. He'd look like a hobo by the time they reached their hideaway. He was determined, however, to appear confident, concerned, willing to listen, and worth talking to. He had to have some authority.

He had to stop listening to Connie calling his name over and over. What was she thinking now? How late had it gotten? Were they on that plane?

The sun on his face told him it was late afternoon and they'd reached another clearing. The sound suggested an opening on the side of the mountain— the hideout. "Just don't let it be a cave," Nick prayed.

He heard a door open. A hand shoved him over the threshold. Someone unlocked his cuffs. He reached up cautiously for the blindfold.

"Go ahead, English."

It was a bunker, cement walls covered in places with cheap paneling, a large table and chairs, a radio against the wall. A second room held cots and not much else. No cells that he could see. Glancing through the open door, he saw the ground drop away to the valley floor far below.

"You drink."

It was a statement, not an offer. Someone handed Nick a jigger of koa-pora. He was sorely tempted to down it in one go. He sipped it, raising the glass to the Colonel. "Very decent of you."

"You are a valuable hostage."

"I prefer to think of myself as a negotiator."

"Your government will do that."

Careful, Nick thought, no sense making the man lose face too soon. He kept an encouraging smile on his face. "The British are quite reasonable—after a fashion. They'll want to make a show of resisting you, but nothing they say can prevent you and me from discussing options."

"You have no power here."

"Surely we can speak."

"You say the wrong thing, we will kill you." It was all done in such a silky tone, Nick could have sworn he was talking to another diplomat. The atmosphere grew chillier. "For your sake, Mr. Atwell, you'd better hope the British desire your release."

"They will. Given time."

"Given time, people grow old and die. On the other hand, some people never grow old."

"You wouldn't want to harm your hostage."

"Not if he is as valuable as he led us to believe. If he is not, where is the harm?"

Plenty to me, Nick thought. He had to stall, to be sure Connie and her father were out of the country before he dropped any more little bombshells.

He poked a finger in the empty pocket where his handkerchief had been, recalling Connie's joyful tears when he'd handed it to her. But that vision couldn't distract him from the blank stares of people who killed as easily as they ate or slept.

"On the other hand," he said, "you may win your war and let me go."

The Colonel smiled. This time his tea-stained teeth didn't show.

Eleven

Connie clutched the handkerchief in her hand. Toreador red was hard to miss. Ambassador Whitcraft did his best not to look at it.

"We are rather helpless, you must see that."

"I *must* have an answer. One of your own people is a hostage. You can't sit there and say it's out of your hands!"

The ambassador directed a pained glance at the letter unfolded before him. He sent a pleading look to his latest secretary-for-public-relations-disasters. "George, could you, uh—"

"Happy to help." George took a deep breath and meandered to the window, lifting one or two heavy red flowers off the balcony railing. "Miss Hennessy, do you know what a renegade is?"

"Do you know what loyalty is?"

George didn't turn, speaking to the view. "He's done this of his own accord. This is not something we can undo."

"You can help him."

"How?"

Connie strode over to him. No way was she going to sit in a sticky leather chair while Whitcraft hid behind his massive teak desk and Cunningham looked down his nose at Lampura City. "You could send in a rescue squad."

"And risk how many lives? Including his?"

"Give me some kind of authorization," Paul said, stepping forward. "Okay it with the Americans and I'll handle the details. We've got plenty of intelligence from Connie's father on where they might be located."

"Might be?" George asked quietly.

"Are," Connie insisted. "Give Paul some men and let him go."

"We have procedures for this sort of thing."

"What sort of thing?" Connie was fed up with diplomatic niceties.

"What to do if embassy personnel are taken hostage," George replied mildly. "Sir?"

"Huh?" Whitcraft followed George's gaze to the unmarked manila folder which held the note. He cleared his throat and read: In response to this incident, there'd be no negotiating, no ransom, no armed assaults. Business would carry on as usual.

Whitcraft took off his reading glasses. "I'll have to practice that a few times before I read it to the press, eh, George?"

Before Connie could voice her outraged indignation at the impersonality of it all, George held up a palm.

"This was the note Nick asked you to deliver to me. He planned it this way."

Connie felt an all-too-familiar helplessness grip her. After making love to her, Nick had sat in their hotel room calmly writing out a press release almost guaranteed to get himself killed.

"He loves you quite a bit," George said, his mild voice intruding gently on her agonized thoughts. "That may be some consolation."

"It isn't." Her knees shook as she stepped toward

the door. She had to think, to go back to the hotel and convince herself her father was still there, he was real, he was back. But nothing had changed. She couldn't rest while someone she loved was in chains.

Paul took her arm as they hurried down the marble stairs. Nick had once carried her up these stairs. He'd once covered her body with his, in this building, shielding her from bombs and bullets and worry, loving her tenderly, fiercely.

If this was love, he could have it. She wanted no part of noble self-sacrifice. She was a fighter. There had to be a way.

"Miss Hennessy?"

The soft voice took a moment to penetrate. Connie gripped Paul's arm as they stopped on the embassy steps.

George came up behind her. "I wished to return Nick's statement to you."

She put it in her purse. "Is that all?"

"He's left you very few alternatives. I know he would have wanted you on that plane."

"Do you think I'm going?"

Smiling faintly, he shook his head. "We don't always do what we should, but we do what we can." He bowed and retreated into the embassy.

Connie muttered a word that made her ex-husband's mouth drop open. "Is that any way to talk?"

She almost laughed, then closed her eyes and sagged against him. "Bad language is the least of my worries."

"What are we going to do about this crazy diplomat of yours?"

"You tell me."

"How'd it go?"

Back at the hotel, there was nothing Connie could

say to her father without bursting into tears. "You should be resting."

"I've been resting for ten years. I want to *do* something."

Connie couldn't have agreed more. She paced side by side with her father, restless, furious, grief-stricken all at once.

"There's a note," her father said when he thought she could handle it. He nodded at the desk.

Connie's heart fluttered. She kicked the suitcase out of the way as she raced to the desk. "He must have written it when he came up here and packed my clothes."

Scanning Nick's sloping handwriting, her mouth drew into a taut line. "Don't you 'chin up' me, you British twit!" She crumpled it in her fist.

To her surprise, Paul laughed.

"This is funny?"

"You don't seem bowled over by his gesture."

"I have a few choice words for Nick Atwell concerning bravery and honor. And he's going to hear them straight from the horse's mouth. Right?"

Her father and her ex-husband stared at her.

"Right?"

Paul balanced himself on both feet, his hands loose at his sides, his eyes searching the room as if for bugging devices. "You got an idea?"

"*I* do." Her father lifted the blotter off the desk and withdrew another sheet of paper. "I drew this from memory while you two were at the embassy. Think you could locate this bunker?"

Paul and Connie crowded around. Finally Paul shook his head, crushing Connie to his side in a bear hug. "Not at night. We'd need better coordinates than that."

"Or a guide," her father said.

Connie's eyes grew wide. "No way. You two are *not* going up there alone." She kicked off her sandals and stuffed her feet into jogging shoes, muttering all the while. "I can see it now. Nick up there, Dad taken hostage again, Paul in chains. Does every man I love have to risk his life all the time?"

"Only the ones who love *you*, kid."

Connie hugged her father tight. "Then take me along. Paul, please."

He fiddled with the envelope George Cunningham had handed them coming out of the embassy. Frowning, he opened it and withdrew more than the statement. An aerial map of the mountains was enclosed, various routes marked in red.

"Think George put it in there by mistake?" Connie asked.

"I don't think that man does anything by mistake."

"Maybe he wants us to go after Nick."

"Maybe it's our necks, not his."

"It's Nick's." Connie put her hand on his arm. "Paul, I know I have no right to ask—"

"Don't cry and don't apologize. You did enough of that when we were married. You know I'd do just about anything for you."

"Including coming halfway around the world because I needed you."

"Don't twist the knife. I've learned to live with it stuck in my heart like that."

"Will you lead a raid?"

"With you and your father in tow?"

"With these maps, and Dad's firsthand knowledge and your expertise—"

"And your determination. You really love this guy."

"After I wring his bloody neck, I'm going to marry him."

All right, so they were going to kill him. Nick knew all along that was a possibility, he just hadn't thought they'd get around to it so soon.

The ambassador's dinnertime statement to the

press was very convincing. Very ably written, too, if he did say so himself. It made the government's position indisputably clear: There'd be no negotiations for his release.

Seated by the shortwave radio in the rebel's outpost, Nick silently thanked George for the timing of Whitcraft's announcement; Connie had to be out of the country by now. If he wanted to live until her plane touched down in Singapore, he'd better start talking. "Colonel, might I say something?"

The Colonel had ceased giving him flinty smiles midway through the ambassador's statement. "Final words are traditional."

Nick cleared his throat. Freedom, democracy, compromise, it didn't matter what he said as long as they let him keep talking. So he gave them an earful of "wait and see," a page and a half of "prudence and patience," a dollop of Churchill, and a dose of John Stuart Mill.

The room was stifling hot. The attention of the soldiers who spoke no English faded fast. Bemused, the Colonel filled an ashtray with cigarette butts. "Are you finished, Englishman?"

He would be if he answered that. "I wished to say a few more words on the art of compromise."

"Give us the telephone number of the British Embassy first, please."

"May I ask why?"

"So we can tell them where to find your body."

Nick turned the shot glass around in his fingers. It had been empty a long time. "I haven't quite finished."

"You have."

"Then I wish to write a letter."

"To whom?"

He paused. "A woman."

The Colonel and one soldier who apparently spoke English sneered.

A gun swung Nick's way. He'd seen the way an automatic weapon could cut a person in two at close range. It made more sense when they led him outside to do it.

The early evening air was heavy with the scent of blossoms and the odor of rotting vegetation. Hardscrabble mountain soil ground beneath his shoes. Sunset illuminated the valley below, koa-pora vines crawling across it. From this height, they resembled the beautifully curved Lampuran alphabet.

They *were* an alphabet. Dark shapes of women came in from the edge of the field, turning meaningless shapes into words, spelling out warnings to the men in the mountains.

"So that's how you communicate," Nick exclaimed. "No radios to jam, no intercepted orders. The old woman organizes all of it."

The Colonel acknowledged Nick's flattery, his composure dissolving as he read the message below. The men around him grew agitated.

Nick repeated it aloud. "'Premier fleeing.' If that's true—"

"Rumors," the Colonel replied.

Nick seized his chance. "By releasing your best-known hostage, you've made yourselves look powerful enough not to need one. The government is unnerved. Your assaults have already weakened it—"

"If we strike now, we win," the Colonel said flatly. "Unfortunately, that gives me no time to hear the rest of your speech." Issuing orders, he hurried into the bunker.

While the soldiers prepared to head for the city, two others hustled Nick around the back.

"Wait a minute," he argued. "There's no sense doing this now, your war is almost over." He had no intention of becoming the final casualty.

On the other hand, he had very little say in it.

Twenty yards distant where the jungle overtook the yard, they shoved him into a shed smothered by foliage. They locked his ankles into two iron rings cemented in the floor and slammed the door.

"We execute you at dawn," one said. "We have no time now." They retreated to the bunker. The sounds of Jeeps roaring down the mountain followed soon after.

Alone, Nick listened to the darkness as the room grew smaller. The shed was damp and suffocating. He couldn't panic. He loosened his tie, then his collar, then reached for his handkerchief—

He'd given it to Connie.

He concentrated on her, willing his heart to slow. When it didn't, he pretended it raced at the memory of her kiss, many kisses, the first by the elevator, the cramped and cranking hotel elevator, which reminded him of the airless stainless steel one in the capitol building.

"No," he ordered himself. "Think of her." The way she'd playfully nipped his ear last night. The way she'd screamed his name when Paul had driven her away.

"You drove her away," his said aloud. "You believed every bad thing anyone's ever said about you and wouldn't let her believe otherwise."

A trickle of sweat stung the corner of his eye. He blinked it open. He could make out one tiny window opposite the door. The chain prevented him from reaching it. He examined his cell by touch, discovering a half dozen shovels against one wall. He supposed he could bash one of his captors over the head when they came to get him.

He supposed they'd want him to dig his own grave.

Harsh breaths hurried out of him. He steadied his pulse. Think of something else, like Connie. Like her perfume.

"Lilacs, wasn't it?" His voice sounded tinny in the

shed. "Miss Hennessy," he murmured, recalling that first day when he'd bent over her chair and, as unobtrusively as possible, inhaled the scent of her shampoo, glimpsed her diamond stud earring.

The door swung open and a guard set a candle, paper, and pen beside him. "Write final wish," he said, and departed.

Nick stared at the paper. A minute ago he'd prayed for light. This flickering illumination only emphasized how close the walls were, how small the space. The ankle chains were sturdy and unbreakable. The tines of a pitchfork useless to pry them off.

He picked up the pen. "Final wish, eh?" Only one, and she wasn't here. He held a lock of hair off his forehead and tried to concentrate. *Connie*, he wrote, then stared at her name. There were a hundred things he had to say, but the image of the soldiers reading them, having a good laugh, and tossing the paper into the grave after him, dried up any flowing phrases he might have begun.

Connie, he wrote again.

"On my signal," Paul said.

Crouching at the edge of the jungle behind the bunker, Connie watched the candlelight flicker and dim in the shed. "What will they do to him?"

"Nothing yet. Your father's watching the road. I've got to circle around the bunker and check access points. I want you to get as close to that shed as you can. Hide in its shadow in case anyone comes out."

She couldn't have asked for better orders. Face blackened by shoe polish, perspiring freely in the black turtleneck Paul had loaned her, Connie quickly lost sight of her ex-husband as he disappeared into the night. She'd had her eye on that candle since they'd arrived. She moved toward it.

Shortly after their arrival most of the rebels had raced toward town. Connie didn't know or care why; Paul estimated six left behind. Music blared from the bunker as they celebrated their anticipated victory. Connie recognized Bob Marley wailing third-world anthems of liberation.

"Play 'No Woman, No Cry,'" Connie muttered, a broken twig snapping underfoot. A chain rustled inside the shed. "Nick?"

Giving up on his letter, Nick pulled his knees up, wrapped his arms around them, and rested his forehead there. "Aural hallucinations," he muttered. He'd pictured her so clearly, he'd conjured her voice whispering his name.

"Nick! What did you say?"

"I said," he replied in a conversational tone, "that claustrophobia takes many forms. I assume you're one of them."

"And I assume you're dead meat if we don't get you out of there."

Nick started. The voice was so faint, he could have sworn he'd invented it to pass the time. Unable to guess the direction, he cautiously got to his feet, leaning one moment toward the door, the next toward the back of the shed and the tiny window.

Hugging the back of the shed, knowing the candlelight might light her up for any perimeter guard to see, Connie raised her head just enough to peek inside. On the other side of the smudged glass, a face met hers. She bit back a scream.

"Connie!" Nick stepped toward her, but the chain stopped him with a jerk. It couldn't stop his hand reaching out for her.

"Keep your voice low," she whispered fiercely, a lump instantly constricting her throat.

She watched a hundred emotions battle for control of his face. To her amazement, indignation won out. He stepped back from the window and peered at the woman he'd called his goddess. A black bandanna hid her auburn hair. Some kind of pitch smeared her milky cheeks, creating the bandit mask of a racoon. Sea-green eyes blinked back tears. Did hallucinations come in disguise?

He tugged the chain until the iron bit into his ankle. He didn't care. "Are you real?"

A muffled sob escaped her. She snaked her arm through the broken windowpane. The sleeve caught on a pointed shard of glass, exposing the long white slope of her arm. Her skin glowed in the candlelight as her fingertips brushed his.

When he let go, she spoke his name. He touched his fingers to his lips then touched hers again. "This is the only way I can kiss you."

She sniffed in an unladylike way. "Don't make me cry, my shoe polish will run."

He forced a grin. Then he moved away.

"I'm appalled," he said in his low diplomat's voice. "Frankly appalled."

"You're what!"

"I can't believe the danger you've put yourself in. Haven't I warned you—"

"Of all the mutton-headed, sheep-for-brains, food-stuffed nonsense! I come up here to save your lousy hide, and this is the thanks I get? I love you!"

"And I love you," he snapped, "that's precisely why I want you out of here. Now."

Connie's fingertips grasped the window ledge. Her toes extended to give her that extra inch—the better to glare at him. "Listen, buster. You make me fall head over heels in love with you when I was convinced only one man's life mattered to me. Then, after you've sworn you don't want to get involved, you save my father single-handedly. *Then* you get yourself trussed up in here like some junkyard dog!"

"If you've come to trade insults, save your breath."

"I'm here to save your life! If you don't mind my

saying so, you look like you need all the help you can get."

He'd needed her and nothing but her, Nick thought. She'd made all the difference in his life—he didn't want her here for his death. "Is Paul with you?" he asked harshly.

"I'm brave, not stupid. He has Dad down the road with a radio in case the rebels return. He also has a personal arsenal that would do a ninja proud."

"He left you a gun, I take it. Give it to me."

Connie ignored his request. Paul had left her one stun grenade with orders to pull the pin should anyone come within twenty feet. Beyond that range, it might not have the blinding, deafening impact it was designed for. Of course, that meant *letting* armed men get that close. She hoped she'd have the nerve.

The Bob Marley tape had run its course. The rebels seemed to be looking for more music.

"Are you all right?" she asked softly.

"I was thinking of you," Nick said.

"Are you mad at me?"

"Mad for you."

"About my coming, I mean."

He sighed and ran a hand through his hair. "Somehow it doesn't surprise me. I'd envisioned you doing something like this since you arrived. For your father. But I'd counted on Paul forcing you onto the plane for Singapore."

"Nick, I never asked you to do this."

Frustrated, he tugged on the chain again. He couldn't get close enough to hold her hand, much less dry her tears. "Hush. Remember your polish."

She laughed in spite of herself. "I'm sure my face is going to break out."

"I'll love you spotty too."

"Do you have to make jokes?"

He shrugged, but that made him lose contact with

her hand. He found it again. "It's easier with you here."

"You're the bravest man I've ever met."

"You'll have to go, you know. Whatever Paul has planned, I don't want you in danger. That was the whole idea."

"The whole idea was rescuing someone I loved. I've pleaded and begged and bargained and watched my mother do the same. I've decided to try action this time."

"I can't approve."

"You're in no position to argue."

"Connie."

"Sh!"

The sounds of the rebels' next anthem increased suddenly as the door to the bunker opened.

Nick released her hand and sat quickly beside the upended pail he'd been using to write his farewell note. He stared at her name, willing her into the darkness of the jungle. He couldn't hear her footsteps under the sound of the soldiers—he didn't know if that meant she'd gone or foolishly stayed. The sound of his heart pounding drowned out everything else. If they found her, it wouldn't disguise a shouted order, nor a gunshot.

He reached for a shovel.

The door swung open. The candle guttered. Slowly, its flame steadied, lighting the Lampuran in the doorway. "You come."

The hairs on the back of his neck prickled. Connie hadn't gone, he knew it. She was no more than a few feet away on the other side of that wall. If they took him behind the shed to execute him, they'd find her. He had to lead them the other way, even if it meant running in the opposite direction. Most people wouldn't consider a bullet in the back brave, but if it meant distracting them from Connie, he'd have little choice.

"Where are we going?" He asked in English, for Connie's ears.

Before he could repeat it in Lampuran, the guard replied in passable English. "Inside."

Away from the shed.

Nick nodded as they unlocked his chains.

Twelve

The rebels had shut the tape deck down to listen to another announcement on the shortwave radio as Ambassador Whitcraft briefed the sparse press corps arrived to cover the latest rebellion. The English-speaking soldier, embarrassed at his inability to translate for his comrades, shoved Nick toward the receiver.

"Tell us what he says, imperialist dog."

Nick stretched to full height. "Excuse me, but we were imperialists before you lot knew what the word meant."

The soldier spit on the floor. "We should be fighting, not guarding."

"Haven't had your share of killing, eh?" He'd had *his* share with the first body he'd seen by the road-side three years ago. The sight had kept him in Lampura. Diplomacy mattered; one resolved one's problems, one didn't exterminate them.

Nevertheless, Nick translated the gist of Whit-craft's message into Lampuran for his captors. "The ambassador says the Premier has boarded the last plane out. The government is in the hands of the people. Looks like you've won."

Five soldiers cheered and shouted. Nick's interrogator grew surly. "It's a trick!"

"The ambassador wouldn't lie."

"You would."

Nick grit his teeth. If this degenerated and Paul felt the need of a surprise attack, he and Connie would be facing alert and intense men—all better armed. "Then keep me prisoner until morning. Or until your leader gets himself on the radio."

"Maybe we kill you now. Then go fight."

The promise of battle garnered a few eager nods.

Nick seized a bottle of koa-pora and poured himself a shot glass full. "A toast," he said in Lampuran. "As a sign of fellow feeling and Great Britain's desire to accommodate itself to whichever government is in the best interest of the people, gentlemen, I give you the new Lampuran nation."

It was a mouthful for a man with his mind on other things, like protecting the woman he loved from charging in, but if Nick couldn't *talk* his way out of this, he just might be able to drink his way out.

Withdrawing every local dollar bill from his wallet, he scattered them on the table. "Let's drink to peace."

They got that part. Fetching four dusky bottles of koa-pora, the celebrating soldiers poured. Nick winked at his suspicious friend and downed two fingers of the fruity drink. It raced to his stomach like honey, settling like lava.

"Another," he offered. "To your Colonel for his brilliant leadership. Above all, to foot soldiers like you, without whose dedication all Lampura would remain in shackles."

After three more toasts he could have saluted Walt Disney and they'd have drunk. "To women," he said at last. "To beautiful, loyal, constant women."

They leered and emptied every bottle.

Nick imagined what their wavering guns must look

like to outside observers, but there was no dampening their elation now.

"Deuced hot in here, wouldn't you say?" Someone obligingly opened the door by wedging a chair in it. "Thanks." He poured himself the next drink, considering carefully. He wanted to say this loud and he wanted to say it right, in English. "True love, gentlemen. And the strength of women who know its worth."

An elbow jammed between two of Nick's ribs. The elbow was a Colt .45.

Nick lowered his arm to his side. It had been an effort not to jerk it down, considering how ticklish he was there. Connie had discovered that only a handful of nights ago. He turned a grim smile on the man to his left.

The surly soldier smiled. "You lie, Englishman, you die."

It wasn't a matter of saving his own hide; he had to prevent Connie and Paul from doing anything rash. The other revelers had taken their seats around the table, or stumbled into them. "I assure you, you've won."

"I'd rather fight."

"Fight or kill?"

He grinned. "We go outside. I'll say you tried to escape."

Nick swallowed bile and washed it down with koa-pora.

"Are you drunk enough to die, Englishman?"

Not by a long shot. The way alcohol affected him, he never would be. "To Connie," he said, lifting his glass. Just in case.

The stun grenade slipped in Connie's sweat-drenched palms, the ring jingling softly. "You've got to do it, Paul."

"I'd like to take the mean-looking one out before we go in, but he's standing too close to Nick."

"Let me use this."

"Did you warn Nick it was coming?"

"No." The word shimmered out on a guilty whisper.

The opportunity to talk to him while he was a captive, to touch him, had taken her completely by surprise. She hadn't known what to say. Separated again, watching him entertain his executioners, the words finally came to her. She had to get him out!

Paul ducked, throwing an arm out to hold her back against the wall as the door opened slightly, noise and music tumbling out. No one followed. A chair wedged it open.

"What *did* you two talk about?" Paul asked at last.

"I told him I loved him."

"I think he knows that."

Did he?

"Go!"

For a few precious seconds, Paul's command didn't penetrate.

"Go!" he ordered as the soldier stepped away from Nick and waved his gun toward the door.

Connie crept to the door, her legs wobbly but her resolve firm. Just as Paul had instructed her during Nick's endless toasts, she pulled the pin from the grenade, threw it through the opened door, and dove for the ground, her eyes shut tight, her hands clamped over her ears.

The ground shook. Seconds dragged by. The acrid smell of explosives and the concussion in her ears told her the grenade had worked. Paul tugged on her arm, then raced into the bunker, rifle in hand. Connie followed.

Bodies tilted in their chairs like puppets with their strings cut. One man writhed on the floor. Paul appeared in the doorway to the bedroom, having swept the bunker for other soldiers and found none.

"You said it wouldn't kill anyone," Connie shouted over the ringing in her ears.

Paul removed a gun from the writhing soldier's fist. "They aren't dead, they're stunned and drunk!"

"Drunk!" The whine in her ears droned like a jet's engines. Suddenly her eyes grew wide as she scanned the passed-out "casualties." "Where's Nick?"

Paul avoided her panicked look.

She ran past him into the bedroom. "Where is he?"

"He was here a minute ago." The banality of the phrase sounded hollowly in the room. Paul pointed with his rifle. "That's the only exit."

Connie raced outside. Paul reached her before she could take a second step. "That blast will alert every rebel on the mountain."

"They're all gone. Where is he, Paul?" Seizing his shirt, she felt the tiny electrical jolt of his silent walkie-talkie signaling in his breast pocket.

Paul answered. "Yeah, Bill?"

Connie barely made out her father's voice as he warned of an approaching vehicle.

"We gotta get out of here." Paul shoved the .45 in her hand, pulling her behind him.

Too late. The headlights of a Jeep barely missed them as they ducked around the corner of the building. They flattened themselves against the concrete as the Jeep came to a halt outside the open door.

Steps crunched toward them. Connie needed two shaking hands to hold the .45. Her finger stretched for the trigger. Paul leapt around the corner in a crouch, rifle aimed and ready. Connie pointed the .45 at the first thing she saw.

Nick stood in the slanting light of the doorway, tie

askew, jacket rumpled, shot glass in his hand. "Ah, there you are. Care to join me in a drink?"

All the way down the mountain Connie gripped the .45 to her thigh. Paul drove. Her father sat in the passenger seat. She and Nick sat in back, as far apart as humanly possible.

"Don't even think about it," she'd snarled as he'd hopped in beside her.

Nick straightened his tie. "I saw the grenade roll in; I wasn't about to wait for it to go off. So I slugged my trigger-happy friend and ran for it."

"Do you really think we'd use a real grenade with you standing there?"

"I'm a diplomat. One grenade looks pretty much like another to me."

Connie scoffed. Every word made hideously perfect sense.

Nick continued in that sane, eminently sensible manner that made her want to scream. "Once outside, I saw the two of you face down on the ground, seeing no evil, hearing no evil, and decided to sprint for the only available vehicle, just in case we needed a quick getaway."

Connie squeezed the butt end of the .45 until the grip pattern dented her hands. "How can you be so damn calm?"

"You're here. We're all free. Everything's all right."

"I almost shot you!" She knew she was shouting by the strain on her vocal cords. Her lungs ached, her stomach turned over at the slightest bump in a road that was all bumps, and Nick wouldn't stop smiling.

He eased the gun out of her hands and pulled her stiff shoulders into the crook of his arm. "It's over," he said.

"Yes, it is," she replied, burying her face against his chest. "Yes, it is." He'd done all this for her. She couldn't let him do anything that dangerous again, not for her sake. She couldn't let him go on loving her.

"Your Dad's sharing my room tonight," Paul said as they stood outside Connie's door in the Imperial Hotel. "You get some rest."

Rest? Connie wasn't sure she'd ever unwind. They'd dropped Nick off at the embassy. She hadn't said good-bye. She hadn't been able to say anything.

"Con?" Paul smudged some of the black off her chin. "If it can't be me, I guess there's no one I'd rather see you with than Nick Atwell."

Accepting his hug, she smiled, then walked into her room and headed straight for the bathroom. Washing off the polish, stripping off the turtleneck to the plain satin camisole she wore beneath it, she heard low male voices murmur in the hall. The door to her room opened and closed. He didn't have to say anything; she knew it was Nick.

She buried her face in a towel, as if it held the words she'd have to say. She'd gained her father and lost the man she loved, all in one night. Could one heart hold two emotions that big? Not without breaking.

He was seated at the desk when she came out, one leg crossed over the other at the ankle, his arm casually canted on the back of the chair. He looked as if he'd taken a quick shower, his hair damp and shiny black. He'd put on a clean white shirt and tan slacks. He hadn't changed a thing.

Connie glanced at the desk where he'd written his farewell. She glanced at the bed where he'd made love to her, where he'd lied to her. *Where you convinced him to free your father.*

All the way down the mountain she'd rehearsed a nonstop tirade on drinking and fools, knights and jackasses—all the things she'd never been able to unload on the calm, collected diplomats who'd stood in her way. She wouldn't need any of it now, thanks to Nick. Her father was free.

But she had another speech that demanded a hearing, about responsibility and sacrifice and what's expected of a daughter and what's simply too much to ask, even of a man who loves you.

"Are you all right?" he asked softly.

She draped the towel over the end of the bed and tried to speak. If he'd been the calm one, the reassuring one, she might have said it all. If he'd been his usual jaunty, imperturbable self, if he hadn't marched across the room and clasped her to him as if he couldn't wait to hold her, couldn't live without her, it might have worked.

But desperation and Nick were new to her. She'd never guessed how strong he'd been through all of this until he crushed her in his arms. "You're here." His voice was as grainy as sandpaper. "God, I love you."

What could a woman who didn't deserve it say to that? "I love you too."

Words poured out of both of them, crossing like the undertow beneath the tide rushing and crashing on a beach only to be replaced by more.

"You could have been killed!"

"I could say the same for you," he answered hoarsely. "I wanted you safe from the first, and you—"

"I wanted my father saved. That didn't mean you had to—"

"And what were you doing, pulling this commando stuff—"

"Don't you ever—"

"—do that again."

"I don't intend to."

"I should say not."

She ran her fingers through his hair and held his

head in her hands. "Get this notion out of your head that you're not brave enough or resolute enough or that you're—"

"Unreliable?"

"Yes! You're one heck of a hero and if nobody sees that, they're blind." She took a deep breath. "I told you you didn't have to rescue my father to make me love you. You didn't believe me."

"Surely that's my fault."

"No! I refused to see it. I knew you were taking all sorts of risks for me, and I did nothing to stop you. If I accept your love, you'll never know if it was payment for what you've done."

"Was it?"

A chill descended on her skin. She'd never loved anyone more. She'd never been less able to say it. Even when her father was held captive, she'd sent her love to him in her imagination every night, along with her prayers. With Nick in front of her, she couldn't get the words out.

"Then that is all you wanted?"

She wrapped her arms tight around her waist. "I wanted to love you. The way any woman loves a man, for who he is and what he is. Not for what you could do for me."

Surrounded by rebel guns, he hadn't sounded half so tense. "And now you've found you don't love me?"

"I don't want to."

"That isn't the same."

"Nick, please."

"Do you love me?"

There was nothing diplomatic about his grip on her arms, nothing tactful about the way he held her to his body, refusing to let her look away. "Tell me. Tell me!"

"I love you. I would have loved you anyway."

"Then why are you putting me through this?"

"Because you'll want me to stay." She touched her

fingers to his lips. "This isn't negotiable, Nick. I can't live in fear for the people I love. I can't go through this again."

Nick's breast pocket was empty. He had no handkerchief to stem her tears. "Now I'm *too* brave."

"If anything happened to me, to us, to our children, you'd be out there risking your neck—"

"Naturally."

"No! It's not natural. People shouldn't have to worry every morning if the people they love will come home to them at night. I've seen the parts of town you wander around, the informants you talk to."

"The revolution's over."

"For now. What's to stop government soldiers from taking to the hills next?" She hiccuped and laughed in spite of her tears. "I want you the way I first met you, unwilling to get involved, unwilling to pull any daring stunts. Sensible."

He shook his head and ran a thumb across her cheek. "Not about you, Connie. I'll never be sensible about you."

"Thank you." She meant for everything, for more than two paltry words could ever express. "I'm sorry."

Something about the way she held herself prevented him from holding her, reaching her. She was as alone as she'd been that first day in the embassy, but the battle she fought now was against him and her own feelings.

Try as he might, he saw no way to soothe her pain. He let her go. He said, "That's it, then." He managed a reasonable good-bye. He got as far as the door. "There is one more thing. I'm afraid you're going to have to come with me."

"Nick."

He held up a hand. "I feel the same way you do; as long as you're on Lampura, I won't be able to sleep for fear something might happen to you. Come stay in the embassy. We'll get you on a plane out of here tomorrow." He hefted her suitcase in one hand. "I've sent your father and Paul over there already."

"Always thinking ahead," she smiled, her face smeared with tears.

"Apparently not far enough."

Thirteen

Connie was sleeping in his bed by the time Nick returned to his apartment in the embassy. He'd been briefing the ambassador on his evening in the mountains, receiving reprimands, citations, marching orders. He was too tired to think.

As for Connie Hennessy, if she believed that the slinky top and skimpy panties were more modest than what she usually wore in his bed, she must have been out on her feet too. He'd seen her in nothing at all on too many hot tropical nights to be fooled. Satin and Connie, sheets and Connie, hell, blackface and a baggy turtleneck—anything or nothing on Connie, aroused him.

Her trembling hands aiming a .45 at him over Paul's shoulder had almost killed him.

No wonder she wanted to get away.

He gingerly sat on the bed, smoothing back her hair, watching her breasts rise and fall in the soft light of dawn. He'd had the world fooled for a long time about his character—he'd even fooled himself. Connie saw through him, always had. But not this time.

She didn't see he had no intention of risking his life now that he had something worth living for. She couldn't see how safe he planned on keeping her, her father, any children they might have. She couldn't see that no matter what she said or did, he'd love her forever.

He unbuckled his belt, then got off the bed to slip off his slacks. His shoes hit the floor with soft thuds, the socks followed. In minutes he was beside her. He inhaled her shampoo, tasting dried tears on her cheeks.

She awoke when his mouth sought hers. A warm liquid tongue met his, parting his lips. He took it in, sharing a kiss like the night, the warm lagoon, a pulse pressing and seeking and retreating. A kiss like being alive.

Before either of them could speak, Nick embraced her, his body lean and hard against her softness, her legs twining around him of their own accord. Her body bowed to his, arching as he stretched the length of her, fitting himself to her, finding her in the dark all over again.

"Shh," he murmured against the convulsive throb of her throat. "Don't cry."

"I love you so much. But we can't—"

"We can."

He could have slipped inside her. He knew by the way she panted his name that she needed him. He knew by the honey coating his tip that she would take him in. The emotions were hard, the loving would be easy—and unprotected.

"Do you want me to?" he asked, knowing she understood as he pressed forward, slick and taut. He looked down into her eyes.

"Yes," she breathed.

"Connie."

No more words than that. She let him love her. They risked it all, their lives, the life they might create together. If she would give him this, how could she walk away?

He lost the words. Promises went unsaid. Loving

had imperatives all its own. Passion seized them and they rode it through the night, swept under and swept away. He couldn't have loved her more. Given a hundred years, he'd never love her less.

Almost dawn. Connie cuddled against him, resting her cheek to his heartbeat. In the sultry morning heat their bodies grew slick wherever they touched. Neither seemed to mind.

"Did I tell you I turned in my resignation?" Nick began.

Connie felt the thump of a heartbeat contradicting his casual tone. "And?"

"George wouldn't accept it, wouldn't even hand it in to the ambassador."

"Why not?"

"He said I was transferred. Paperwork's already in the pipeline."

"Where to?"

"London. I'll be working in the Crypt."

"What?" She sat up, hair spilling across them both, her breast brushing his side. "But you hate small spaces! They can't do that to you."

Nick chuckled. "Cryptography Department, encoding, decoding. It seems I'm not cut out for the finer aspects of diplomacy. They're giving me something I can live with."

We can live with, Connie thought, a glimmer of hope shooting through her like a star to wish upon. "Why didn't they do this sooner? Why didn't you ask for it?"

"Code work requires the highest security clearance there is. Until George amended my record, I couldn't have gotten in."

"All the black marks are erased?"

He slanted his fingertips across her forehead. "Like your makeup."

Connie placed her hand where her cheek had been. She wanted to feel him answer, to see him, to hear him all at once.

"What is it?" he asked.

"You once said you wanted to save people. Do you really want to leave?"

"I've saved enough people for one lifetime. The people I love."

Connie tried to smile, really she did. "Nick."

For the second time in twenty-four hours his life depended on saying the right thing, reaching for any word or phrase to make her see. "You risked your neck for me. You can't convince me you don't love me."

"I wouldn't try."

"Then don't leave."

"We have to. The plane. The arrangements."

"I meant without me. Stay with me. Here, in London, anywhere in the world. I need you." He propped himself on an elbow, running his free hand through his hair. "I honestly can't say how I'd survive otherwise."

She laughed. "Is this a proposal?"

"Do you want me down on one knee?"

Her smiled faded. In a flash Connie remembered their encounter with the rebels in town, the rifle butt slamming into Nick's abdomen, the way he'd dropped to his knees.

"No! I never want to see you on your knees again, not for my sake."

Another refusal. Nick cast about, his arguments getting weaker by the minute. "You'd like London. I'm sure you would. I hope *I* will. It's been a while. No heat but—"

"Lots of rain."

"Where did you say you lived in America?"

"California."

"Well, London doesn't have any of that incessant sunshine. Maybe you'd like cloudy days."

She looked doubtful.

He nattered on. "One can curl up with a good book on a cloudy day."

"Or a good woman," she murmured.

His heart stalled, then stopped altogether. "Yes."

"This good woman," she said, the hint of a smile curving the corner of her mouth.

"Will you?"

"Will I what?"

She was teasing him now. She knew damn well what he wanted, and, though his heart didn't entirely believe it yet, she planned on giving it to him. "Will you marry me?"

"I love you," she said, as if that explained everything.

Nick wasn't taking any more chances. He took that as a yes. Then he took Connie as only a lover can.

"Is there some reason," he asked an hour later when they were hopelessly tangled in the sheets and too tired to do anything about it, "some earthly reason why you couldn't have come right out and said you'd marry me?"

Connie smiled, a trace of remembered pain in her eyes. But the smile lingered as if she'd brave anything to keep it there. "I couldn't love you any more if I tried," she whispered. "That's why I can't risk losing you."

"Then marry me."

"And when all this is over? Won't you get bored when there's no danger anymore?"

"What about you? With no causes to fight for—"

"There'll always be causes. Unfortunately. Amnesty International and the Red Cross have lists of people who need someone to take up their cause."

"A one-woman crusade. You're not leaving it behind, then?"

"I have so many contacts. I could be of use; it wouldn't be just for me or my family." She blushed a soft pink in the full light of morning. "But I need a life of my own too. I'm afraid you'd get bored with what I really want."

"Which is?"

"A home. A family." She snuggled closer, kicking sheets out of the way to hold him tight. "I want the most boring, normal life there is. Dinners on the table. Vacations at the beach. I want to snuggle on the couch and watch rented movies. To have you come home and complain about your day."

"I'd never complain about coming home to you."

"Are you sure?"

"As sure as that ocean is wide. As sure as London is a world away from here."

"You never told me you were a poet too."

"You should see some of my limericks."

He chuckled at the rhymes that came to him. He'd have to clean them up for Connie. Then again, maybe not. She saw him as he was, always had. Always would. She believed in him and that's all he needed.

They jumped at a bird shrieking on the balcony rail. Then they laughed, and made love, and made promises that would last when Lampura was far behind them. Her father would live with them. They'd start a family. Their tropical honeymoon would begin today.

Saucy and sweet, fragrant and honeyed, the aromas of the day tangled with the flowers overgrowing the balcony and the salty scent of the sea as sunrise warmed the bed.

Outside the window, the city woke up. At the end of the Avenue de Charles de Gaulle, the Indian Ocean lapped at a sugary beach, the pounding swell of the water mimicking the crests of love, the private beaches all lovers lay upon. Hushed waves answered hushed words. In a hotel room on an island at the end of the world, love was being made, a love to span continents and last a lifetime.

THE EDITOR'S CORNER

What could be more romantic than Valentine's Day and six LOVESWEPT romances all in one glorious month! Celebrate this special time of the year by cuddling up with the wonderful books coming your way soon.

The first of our reading treasures is **ANGELS SINGING** by Joan Elliott Pickart, LOVESWEPT #594. Drew Sloan's first impression of Memory Lawson isn't the best, considering she's pointing a shotgun at him and accusing him of trespassing on her mountain. But the heat that flashes between them convinces him to stay and storm the walls around her heart . . . until she believes that she's just the kind of warm, loving woman he's been looking for. Joan comes through once more with a winning romance!

We have a real treat in store for fans of Kay Hooper. After a short hiatus for work on **THE DELANEY CHRISTMAS CAROL** and other books, Kay returns with **THE TOUCH OF MAX,** LOVESWEPT #595, the *fiftieth* book in her illustrious career! If you were a fan of Kay's popular "Hagan Strikes Again" and "Once Upon a Time" series, you'll be happy to know that **THE TOUCH OF MAX** is the first of four "Men of Mysteries Past" books, all of which center around Max Bannister's priceless gem collection, which the police are using as bait to catch a notorious thief. But when innocent Dinah Layton gets tangled in the trap, it'll take that special touch of Max to set her free . . . and capture her heart. A sheer delight—and it'll have you breathlessly waiting for more. Welcome back, Kay!

In Charlotte Hughes's latest novel, Crescent City's new soccer coach is **THE INCREDIBLE HUNK,** LOVE-SWEPT #596. Utterly male, gorgeously virile, Jason Profitt has the magic touch with kids. What more perfect guy could there be for a redhead with five children to raise! But Maggie Farnsworth is sure that once he's seen her chaotic life, he'll run for the hills. Jason has another plan of action in mind, though—to make a home in her loving arms. Charlotte skillfully blends humor and passion in this page-turner of a book.

Appropriately enough, Marcia Evanick's contribution to the month, **OVER THE RAINBOW,** LOVESWEPT #597, is set in a small town called Oz, where neither Hillary Walker nor Mitch Ferguson suspects his kids of matchmaking when he's forced to meet the lovely speech teacher. The plan works so well the kids are sure they'll get a mom for Christmas. But Hillary has learned never to trust her heart again, and only Mitch's passionate persuasion can change her mind. You can count on Marcia to deliver a fun-filled romance.

A globetrotter in buckskins and a beard, Nick Leclerc has never considered himself **THE FOREVER MAN,** LOVESWEPT #598, by Joan J. Domning. Yet when he appears in Carla Hudson's salon for a haircut and a shave, her touch sets his body on fire and fills him with unquenchable longing. The sexy filmmaker has leased Carla's ranch to uncover an ancient secret, but instead he finds newly awakened dreams of hearth and home. Joan will capture your heart with this wonderful love story.

Erica Spindler finishes this dazzling month with **TEMPTING CHANCE,** LOVESWEPT #599. Shy Beth Waters doesn't think she has what it takes to light the sensual spark in gorgeous Chance Michaels. But the outrageous results of her throwing away a chain letter finally convince her that she's woman enough to tempt Chance—and that he's more than eager to be caught in her embrace. Humorous, yet seething with emotion and desire, **TEMPTING CHANCE** is one tempting morsel from talented Erica.

Look for four spectacular novels on sale now from FANFARE. Award-winning Iris Johansen confirms her place as a major star with **THE TIGER PRINCE,** a magnificent new historical romance that sweeps from exotic realms to the Scottish highlands. In a locked room of shadows and sandalwood, Jane Barnaby meets adventurer Ruel McClaren and is instantly transformed from a hard-headed businesswoman to the slave of a passion she knows she must resist.

Suzanne Robinson first introduced us to Blade in **LADY GALLANT,** and now in the new thrilling historical romance **LADY DEFIANT,** Blade returns as a bold, dashing hero. One of Queen Elizabeth's most dangerous spies, he must romance a beauty named Oriel who holds a clue that could change history. Desire builds and sparks fly as these two unwillingly join forces to thwart a deadly conspiracy.

Hailed by Katherine Stone as "emotional, compelling, and triumphant!", **PRIVATE SCANDALS** is the debut novel by very talented Christy Cohen. From the glamour of New York to the glitter of Hollywood comes a heartfelt story of scandalous desires and long-held secrets . . . of dreams realized and longings denied . . . of three remarkable women whose lifelong friendship would be threatened by one man.

Available once again is **A LOVE FOR ALL TIME** by bestselling author Dorothy Garlock. In this moving tale, Casey Farrow gives up all hope of a normal life when a car crash leaves indelible marks on her breathtaking beauty . . . until Dan Farrow, the man who rescued her from the burning vehicle, convinces her that he loves her just the way she is.

Also on sale this month in the hardcover edition from Doubleday is **THE LADY AND THE CHAMP** by Fran Baker. When a former Golden Gloves champion meets an elegant, uptown girl, the result is a stirring novel of courageous love that Julie Garwood has hailed as "unforgettable."

Happy reading!

With warmest wishes,

Nita Taublib

Nita Taublib
Associate Publisher
LOVESWEPT and FANFARE

OFFICIAL RULES TO WINNERS CLASSIC SWEEPSTAKES

No Purchase necessary. To enter the sweepstakes follow instructions found elsewhere in this offer. You can also enter the sweepstakes by hand printing your name, address, city, state and zip code on a 3" x 5" piece of paper and mailing it to: Winners Classic Sweepstakes, P.O. Box 785, Gibbstown, NJ 08027. Mail each entry separately. Sweepstakes begins 12/1/91. Entries must be received by 6/1/93. Some presentations of this sweepstakes may feature a deadline for the Early Bird prize. If the offer you receive does, then to be eligible for the Early Bird prize your entry must be received according to the Early Bird date specified. Not responsible for lost, late, damaged, misdirected, illegible or postage due mail. Mechanically reproduced entries are not eligible. All entries become property of the sponsor and will not be returned.

Prize Selection/Validations: Winners will be selected in random drawings on or about 7/30/93, by VENTURA ASSOCIATES, INC., an independent judging organization whose decisions are final. Odds of winning are determined by total number of entries received. Circulation of this sweepstakes is estimated not to exceed 200 million. Entrants need not be present to win. All prizes are guaranteed to be awarded and delivered to winners. Winners will be notified by mail and may be required to complete an affidavit of eligibility and release of liability which must be returned within 14 days of date of notification or alternate winners will be selected. Any guest of a trip winner will also be required to execute a release of liability. Any prize notification letter or any prize returned to a participating sponsor, Bantam Doubleday Dell Publishing Group, Inc., its participating divisions or subsidiaries, or VENTURA ASSOCIATES, INC. as undeliverable will be awarded to an alternate winner. Prizes are not transferable. No multiple prize winners except as may be necessary due to unavailability, in which case a prize of equal or greater value will be awarded. Prizes will be awarded approximately 90 days after the drawing. All taxes, automobile license and registration fees, if applicable, are the sole responsibility of the winners. Entry constitutes permission (except where prohibited) to use winners' names and likenesses for publicity purposes without further or other compensation.

Participation: This sweepstakes is open to residents of the United States and Canada, except for the province of Quebec. This sweepstakes is sponsored by Bantam Doubleday Dell Publishing Group, Inc. (BDD), 666 Fifth Avenue, New York, NY 10103. Versions of this sweepstakes with different graphics will be offered in conjunction with various solicitations or promotions by different subsidiaries and divisions of BDD. Employees and their families of BDD, its division, subsidiaries, advertising agencies, and VENTURA ASSOCIATES, INC., are not eligible.

Canadian residents, in order to win, must first correctly answer a time limited arithmetical skill testing question. Void in Quebec and wherever prohibited or restricted by law. Subject to all federal, state, local and provincial laws and regulations.

Prizes: The following values for prizes are determined by the manufacturers' suggested retail prices or by what these items are currently known to be selling for at the time this offer was published. Approximate retail values include handling and delivery of prizes. Estimated maximum retail value of prizes: 1 Grand Prize ($27,500 if merchandise or $25,000 Cash); 1 First Prize ($3,000); 5 Second Prizes ($400 each); 35 Third Prizes ($100 each); 1,000 Fourth Prizes ($9.00 each) ; 1 Early Bird Prize ($5,000); Total approximate maximum retail value is $50,000. Winners will have the option of selecting any prize offered at level won. Automobile winner must have a valid driver's license at the time the car is awarded. Trips are subject to space and departure availability. Certain black-out dates may apply. Travel must be completed within one year from the time the prize is awarded. Minors must be accompanied by an adult. Prizes won by minors will be awarded in the name of parent or legal guardian.

For a list of Major Prize Winners (available after 7/30/93): send a self-addressed, stamped envelope entirely separate from your entry to: Winners Classic Sweepstakes Winners, P.O. Box 825, Gibbstown, NJ 08027. Requests must be received by 6/1/93. DO NOT SEND ANY OTHER CORRESPONDENCE TO THIS P.O. BOX.

FANFARE

On Sale in December

THE TIGER PRINCE

☐ 29968-9 $5.50/6.50 in Canada
by Iris Johansen

Bantam's "Mistress of Romantic Fantasy"
author of THE GOLDEN BARBARIAN

LADY DEFIANT

☐ 29574-8 $4.99/5.99 in Canada
by Suzanne Robinson

Bestselling author of LADY GALLANT
and LADY HELLFIRE

"Lavish in atmosphere, rich in adventure, filled with suspense
and passion, LADY DEFIANT is a fitting sequel to
LADY GALLANT. Suzanne Robinson brilliantly captures the
era with all the intrigue, costume, drama, and romance that
readers adore." --*Romantic Times*

PRIVATE SCANDALS

☐ 56053-0 $4.99//5.99 in Canada
by Christy Cohen

A stunning debut novel of friendship,
betrayal, and passionate romance

A LOVE FOR ALL TIME

☐ 29996-4 $4.50/5.50 in Canada
by Dorothy Garlock

One of Ms. Garlock's most beloved romances of all time

FANFARE

The Very Best in Historical Women's Fiction

Rosanne Bittner

_____ 28599-8 EMBERS OF THE HEART $4.50/5.50 in Canada
_____ 28319-7 MONTANA WOMAN $4.99/5.99
_____ 29033-9 IN THE SHADOW OF THE MOUNTAINS $5.50/6.99
_____ 29014-2 SONG OF THE WOLF...........................$4.99/5.99
_____ 29015-0 THUNDER ON THE PLAINS $5.99/6.99

Kay Hooper

_____ 29256-0 THE MATCHMAKER $4.50/5.50

Iris Johansen

_____ 28855-5 THE WIND DANCER $4.95/5.95
_____ 29032-0 STORM WINDS.................................$4.99/5.99
_____ 29244-7 REAP THE WIND $4.99/5.99
_____ 29604-3 THE GOLDEN BARBARIAN $4.99/5.99

Teresa Medeiros

_____ 29047-5 HEATHER AND VELVET $4.99/5.99

Patricia Potter

_____ 29070-3 LIGHTNING $4.99/ 5.99
_____ 29071-1 LAWLESS $4.99/ 5.99
_____ 29069-X RAINBOW......................................$4.99/ 5.99

Fayrene Preston

_____ 29332-X THE SWANSEA DESTINY $4.50/5.50

Amanda Quick

_____ 29325-7 RENDEZVOUS $4.99/5.99
_____ 28354-5 SEDUCTION $4.99/5.99
_____ 28932-2 SCANDAL $4.95/5.95
_____ 28594-7 SURRENDER $4.50/5.50

Deborah Smith

_____ 28759-1 THE BELOVED WOMAN $4.50/ 5.50

Ask for these titles at your bookstore or use this page to order.